ASHLEY REYES

Theirs To Destroy

First published by Dark Hearts Romance 2023

First edition

ISBN: 9798322128755

This book was professionally typeset on Reedsy.
Find out more at reedsy.com

This book is dedicated to all the smut sluts who read my first book, enjoyed the little plot, and still wanted more. I hope I made your smutty hearts happy.

Contents

Trigger Warnings

This book is a DARK romance novel suitable for adults only. This book is not a guide on BDSM or healthy relationships. These men are giant, walking red flags. Male-on-male content is included, so turn back now if you're not into that. This book also contains a huge amount of smut, but, if you've read the first one, then you know that already.

This book contains dark and potentially triggering material and kinks. Including, but not limited to: somnophilia, rape (not committed by MMC), graphic child SA, mentions of trauma, mentions of drug use, drugging, murder, graphic sex, group sex, murder, degradation, assault/harassment, abuse, forced marriage, sword crossing, blood and blood play, forced exhibitionism, kidnapping, bondage, non-graphic mentions of child SA, sex trafficking, chopping off someone's penis. If you feel any have been missed, feel free to contact me on social media.

If you have triggers, please tread carefully. Your mental health matters.

Playlist

Bring Me The Horizon - *Follow You*
Sleep Token - *Alkaline*
RIVALS - *Nobody Loves Me*
Bad Omens - *Just Pretend*
April Jai - *Morally Grey*
Aryia - *Vampire*
Picturesque - *Holding Me Down*
Bryce Savage - *Devil In Her Eyes*
Blindlove - *Bad Timing*
Jim Yosef x RIELL - *Animal*
Conan Grey - *Family Line*
Stileto x Kendyle Paige - *Cravin'*
Steven Rodriguez - *She Knows It*
Ari Abdul - *Worship Me*
SWIM - *Eyes On You*
Nikki Idol - *Lady, Touch Yourself*
Catch Your Breath - *Shame On Me*
Motionless In White - *Eternally Yours*

Cain

Tim was a year younger than me. His family moved in last year, and we became friends. He was my bi-awakening. I had a girlfriend, Samantha, but we didn't do anything except hold hands. When Tim kissed me, I knew I liked boys. But I also knew I still liked girls. I liked Samantha as more than a friend. She gave me butterflies when she held my hand.

Unfortunately, my dad didn't see me kiss Samantha. He saw me kiss Tim. He walked in during our sleepover, and we were under my covers. Nothing had happened beyond kissing yet, but I wanted it to. Kissing him was worth the position I was currently in, locked in a room with some man who reeked of beer, weed, and musk.

"You're going to suck and take so many cocks that you'll get sick of them. No son of mine will be gay," my dad bitterly announced before allowing the man into my room.

"I'm not gay!" I yelled.

I was still small, eleven, and couldn't fight for myself yet. I knew my dad was strictly business and all about the family image, but I had no idea he'd take something like this so far.

1

I didn't think he'd sell out his son's holes for random men. If anyone found out, what would that do to the family image he cared so much about?

"You said I get thirty minutes, right?" the man asked. My dad nodded in confirmation. The man handed him a few hundred-dollar bills before my father shoved me into the room.

"Let's not waste time," the man directed me with a smirk. "You like cock, right? This shouldn't be an issue for you then."

"Not yours," I huffed, crossing my arms around my chest. "I haven't even tried anything beyond kissing yet," I said. I watched as the man's erection grew in his pants.

"So I'll be the first cock you put into your pretty little mouth," he said plainly. It took all my might to keep the bile in my stomach and not all over my room. He pulled down his pants and boxers, exposing himself to me. He wasn't packing anything impressive. "Lucky me getting to use your mouth for the first time. You'll always remember me."

"I'll always remember how much you made me gag," I retorted.

Wrong response.

He tightly gripped my hair in his fist and brought my mouth to his soft cock, rubbing it around my lips until he started to harden. Then, he forced himself past my lips. I tried to keep them closed, but he was forceful. He pushed himself deep into my throat until I gagged around him. It was disgusting, yet I found myself wanting to please him. I didn't like him. I despised him. But I needed practice because I wouldn't let my father ruin things for me. I wouldn't let him destroy me and win. I'd beat him at his own game.

I sucked his cock like I had experience. He only lasted ten minutes despite paying for a half hour with me. He left after, and my father made me strip down and whipped me ten times—one for each minute. All he taught me was to get better so I could make it quicker.

And I never stopped liking men, not even when he made them start fucking me.

Cain

I woke up from my horrid nightmare only to realize I had dozed off in the bed while Wolf paced around the room.

In a few short weeks, life changed. Amelia and Lennox were no longer in our lives. Wolf and I were staying in a cabin an hour away from town. We didn't want to be the ones to tell Lennox about Amelia. We knew she married Lennox's dad, and we hadn't talked to her since. Surprisingly, she refused to speak to us, not the other way around. You'd think we'd ignored the girl who stabbed our friend and married his dad, but we wanted nothing more than to know she was okay and cared for. By now, Lennox knew, but he hadn't contacted either of us since the hospital. We didn't tell him how we saw her at school. She didn't notice we were there, or she wasn't looking for us. He remained at home, recovering. We didn't tell him where we were going, either. He'd put the pieces together soon enough.

"We fucked up, Cain," Wolf reminded me. "I—I need her."

I fell harder for her, but he felt like he could've done more to help her or less to hurt her. He forgot that our girl was strong. She could take everything he did. If not, she would've used her safe word.

Every night, before we went to bed, he paced around the room. The cabin was small, leaving us with one queen bed for our stay. If I wasn't waking up from nightmares, Wolf was. We were fucked from what happened. We lost the girl we were falling for; she stabbed our best friend, and then she married his dad. We still wanted her. We blamed Lennox for most of it. If he told us his plan, we could've stopped it.

I knew she wasn't gone for good, but my brain refused to believe it. Amelia loved us. She chose us. Lennox fucked it up for all of us, and Amelia married his dad out of spite, not out of love. Something odd was going on there, and I'd get to the bottom of it.

"We're going to get her back, Wolf," I uttered the exact words I repeated every night. I didn't know if I was trying to convince him or myself. She probably wouldn't want us back if she thought we were involved in Lennox's plan. We all had a lot to make up for, even without his homecoming game stunt, and we had to do things on our terms.

"I think it's time to get a little revenge on Lennox. Destroy him a little more inside," I suggested.

"And what makes you think we can get to Lennox? What makes you think he gives a shit about any of us?" Wolf questioned.

"Lennox does care. I can tell. He's just bad with feelings. Do you trust me, Wolf?" I asked.

He stopped pacing. I stood before him, placing my hands on his shoulders. I watched as he nodded his head and took a deep breath. "I do," he responded. I grinned. I had this idea for a while, mostly because I knew my little thorn wouldn't care. She'd like it, mainly because we would hurt Lennox. Emotionally, at least. One day, he'd have to wake up and realize he had a heart, and he let it be destroyed by hurting the girl he loved.

First, I had to test Wolf's willingness. I pulled his body to mine and kissed him on the lips. He stood motionless for a moment; then, his lips eagerly gave in to the kiss. He didn't have a problem with me eating his cum, so I assumed he wouldn't have an issue with kissing, either. I was right.

"If you want me to stop anytime, just tell me. I promise I'll listen," I advised him. He nodded.

I pushed him backward until the back of his knees hit the bed, sending him stumbling back to lay on it. He looked at me with a feral look in his eyes. We had both gone without sexual content for a week. It was normal for me before, but not exactly for him. He didn't need it as much as Lennox did.

I pulled my phone out of my pocket and sat it on the bed. I kept my clothes on because it was about Wolf, not me. I crawled over him on the bed, my fingers fumbling with the button on his pants. I pulled his pants down with his boxers, and to my surprise, he was getting hard already. Wolf was large, but I already knew that. We had shared Amelia multiple times. I felt him hitting me through the thin barrier of her wall the first time we took her together. His cum landed on me when we shared her with Lennox. Wolf and I were close; nothing I could do would change that. If it got weird, we'd forget about it.

"Don't worry about the camera," I told him. "It's going to be focused on me, okay?"

I ran my hand up and down his length a few times. I turned the camera to my face, holding it close to see what I was doing to him. I had a plan for the video, one that involved more than masturbating to it repeatedly. I refused to be with anyone who wasn't Amelia, Wolf, or Lennox. My hand would have to do for a while, but we'd win her back eventually.

I took a deep breath to brace myself. Wolf knew about my past and trauma. He knew how hard it was for me to accept that I craved Lennox. How long it took me to give in to the urges I felt. Therefore, he knew it was hard for me to do what I would do. I could tell by the worry in his eyes.

Wolf braced himself on his elbows, looking down at me as I pressed record on the phone and leaned forward, lapsing my tongue around the head of his engorged cock, licking up a bead of precum.

"Oh, fuck, Cain," Wolf groaned.

His approval encouraged me to keep going. I wanted to have him come in my mouth. I wanted to have him moaning beneath me. I wanted to show Lennox he fucked up. Most importantly, I wanted to do this to Wolf because I wanted to, not because someone made me.

I sucked down his length, taking him in my mouth until he hit the back of my throat, then swirling my tongue around the tip again while taking a breather. Wolf was larger than Lennox and anyone I had ever fit in my mouth, but I was determined.

"Treat me like you would anyone else," I demanded. Despite how hard he tried for me, I knew he wasn't used to relinquishing control. He felt like I couldn't handle it, but I would. "Control the situation."

Wolf fell flat from his elbows, his hand wrapping in my hair and tugging. He bucked his hips up, sending his length to the back of my throat and holding me in place while I struggled to breathe. Fuck, it was so fucking hot. He released me seconds later but kept thrusting brutally upward in my throat. The only sounds in the room were Wolf's moaning and my slurping his cock down my throat as I tried to suck each time he roughly pushed in.

"Your mouth feels so fucking perfect, Cain. It's so warm for me. Are you going to take my come down your throat?" Wolf said in a low, deep voice. My eyes rolled. My dick was hard, and I had to keep telling it that it wasn't about us tonight. I moaned my answer around his length. With one hand tugging at my hair, his other gripped the comforter, the veins on his hand further turning me on. I imagined sharing this experience with my little thorn. Seeing me and Lennox together turned her on. We belonged to her as much as we belonged to each other.

I reached between us and started to massage his balls. Wolf's back arched off the bed, sending him deeper into my throat as I gagged.

"Fuuuck, Cain. Holy shit. I'm going to fucking come," he announced, moaning as he spilled into my mouth while buried in the back of my throat. When he finished, his body dropped limp, and the sounds of his heavy breathing filled the air. I pulled away, swallowing every last drop. I leaned down, running my tongue along his sensitive cock to collect the leftover cum. It was my fetish, and he knew it. Wolf let out a low groan while fisting the sheets until his knuckles were white. "Jesus," he muttered. "That felt...incredible."

I stopped the recording and dropped my phone. I sat on my knees, looking at a sweaty, smiling Wolf.

"Are you going to send that to Lennox?" Wolf asked.

"Yes," I answered. "He cares about us, and he cares about Amelia. You'll see. We'll find out when he returns to campus," I explained. We shunned Lennox long enough, ignoring his calls and texts. He was probably spiraling by now. Whereas Wolf and I snuck in to attend classes, Lennox hadn't. We hadn't seen him since the hospital.

What I didn't admit to Wolf was that I planned to send it to Amelia, too.

Amelia

The look on Lennox's face when he found out was priceless yet heartbreaking. I was mainly glad I didn't kill him, even if it was only because I was delighted to see him suffer. It hurt most that Cain and Wolf disappeared, too. Did Lennox run off and join them? Did he go back to his mom's house even though she returned? I had no idea what was happening anymore. I hoped to see Cain watching me everywhere I turned, but I saw him nowhere. Each time I didn't see him, I felt more disappointed. I even pretended I was asleep to see if he'd sneak in. He'd lose his chance in a few days.

My phone vibrated on the end table. It was early in the morning, and I was wrapped undercover and staring at the ceiling. I didn't feel at home in James's house. Thankfully, I slept in a guest bedroom. His mom's house was nice, but his dad's house, which was now mine, too, was on a different level—twice the size, more luxurious.

I had a video message from Cain. I thought about ignoring it, unsure what awaited me, but decided to open it. Holy fuck. The video shocked me. It was Cain giving Wolf a blow job. Neither of them was quiet, which turned me on. I hadn't had a release for days. Usually, I didn't care for masturbation. Now,

I felt like I needed it. I walked over toward my drawer in the dresser, grabbed one of my few vibrators, and brought it back to the bed. I took off my shorts and panties, laid on my back, and spread my thighs wide. I could imagine it was one of them touching me.

I started the video from the beginning. Touching myself wasn't enough anymore. I needed a vibrator on the highest setting to feel anything. I turned it on, moved it between my thighs, and pressed it against my clit. I moaned, watching as Cain took Wolf's cock in his mouth. Cain knew what he was doing, and Wolf was enjoying himself. I loved how my moans mixed in with Wolf's.

I heard the window open and turned off my vibrator. Beyond what the moon illuminated, the room was dark. When I saw the dark, buff shadow, I knew it was Cain. When he walked closer to me, the moonlight shone on his face. The growing stubble on his face told me he wasn't shaving. Where had he been?

"Cain?" I asked in a whisper, sitting in the bed.

He sat at the end of the bed, his eyes trailing from my face down my exposed body.

"Fuck, Amelia. I've missed this sight so much. Once I sent you that video, I had to come see you. Consequences of getting caught be damned," he explained. "I've missed you, Little Thorn."

I debated telling him anything. I couldn't ruin what I had set in motion with Henry. We had a plan to abide by. We had documents to sign next week, so I could do whatever I wanted. Until then, and for the foreseeable future, I had to maintain an image. One of a happy, loving wife. Especially at school, since he was the dean. I debated finishing my degree. I didn't need it, but I liked being at school. I wanted to do something meaningful with my life.

"I…I've missed you, Cain. I—I need you," I told him.

I wanted nothing more than to jump on him and shove him down on the bed. I wanted to mount him and take what I wanted, but it wasn't my place. I needed him to make the move. At the same time, I felt terrible for wanting him. Not because I was married but because I felt shame over wanting one of the men who humiliated me.

Cain crawled toward me on the bed. He crawled on top of me, forcing me on my back. He hovered over me, his face burying in my neck and biting the skin before soothing it with his tongue. "I missed your taste," he mumbled into my neck. His lips found mine, and he kissed me with the most gentle kiss he had ever given me. "I missed your lips." He pulled away and looked me in the eye. "I've missed your fucking soul."

He shifted down to lay between my legs, his eyes looking at my bare pussy with an intense desire I had never seen in him before. It's almost like he'd die if he didn't get a taste.

"I'm not going to fuck you, Amelia," he said, prompting me to pout. He chuckled. "This is all about you. Lay back and enjoy." He dove in, his tongue lapping at the wetness pooled between my legs. His tongue shoved into my entrance, and he spent time slowly fucking me with his tongue. The way his tongue moved was almost like he was eating his friend's cum from me again, but he wasn't. I could tell he was using his skills to say what he verbally wouldn't say. He was rectifying the things he had done in the way he knew how. None of us had healthy relationships to learn from—especially not Cain and I.

I grabbed the bed sheet with one hand and his hair with the other, tugging tightly on both. He pulled his tongue out and quickly replaced it with his curled fingers, his mouth sucking lightly on my clit instead.

"Holy fuck," I said, gripping the sheet tightly so I wouldn't pull out his hair.

"I missed your taste, Little Thorn. Fucking Heaven," he said, his fingers pushing harder and deeper into me, deliciously hitting my G-spot with each thrust. My hips arched off the bed when his tongue started flicking my clit intensely. The movement sent his fingers deeper and pushed my pussy entirely in his face. He responded by moaning against me, sending vibrations to my clit.

"Oh, God, Cain. I missed your tongue so much," I admitted loudly. I hoped tonight wasn't the night Lennox decided to show up again.

"Fuck. I want you to come in my mouth, my good girl. I want to taste you. I want you to clench my fingers and drown me in your sweet come," Cain said hoarsely.

He took his free hand and reached up, pinching my nipple between his fingers.

"Cain!" I yelled. My body tried to move up on the bed, but he held me in place while I writhed beneath his weight. I missed his muscular frame holding me down, how he smelled of cedar wood, how he worshipped and devoured me. But for now, things couldn't go past this night.

"That's right, baby, come undone for me. Scream my name while you come on my tongue," he demanded.

It didn't take long for my body to give in. He went from circles on my clit to a side-to-side motion. My head fell back, my eyes closed, and I orgasmed while screaming his name as he requested. He licked me through my intense orgasm. My body hadn't had a proper, good release since the last time I was with them. I needed it, and it lasted over a minute while I thrashed under him. When it subsided and he pulled away, I looked up. My eyes connected with Lennox's as he stood at the end of the bed. It felt like the bathroom all over again, but the men were reversed. I hadn't heard him come in above my screaming. I also didn't notice his phone recording until then. My eyes widened as panic began to fill me. How could I be so fucking stupid? I could lose everything.

"Wow, stepmom. That certainly doesn't look like my dad," Lennox teased, smirking. "And when he sees this video, if he does, I think he'll agree. Seeing as he's in Europe."

"You already own me with the evidence, Lennox. Another video can't make that worse," I reminded him. Technically, unless I found the evidence he spoke of, I had to do what he said—what all of them said. The thought made me nauseous because they could ruin me. I wasn't sure where any of us stood.

Cain stood up from the bed, his massive hard cock apparent in his jeans. He grabbed the phone from Lennox's hand and tossed it to me. When Lennox tried to come toward me, Cain held him back. Then, he decked Lennox in the face, sending him to the ground.

I erased the video before turning on my lamp. Lennox moved to a sitting position and looked between Cain and me. He probably didn't expect Cain to do that, much like I didn't. Then, I noticed the black eye, bloody lip, and bloody knuckles on Lennox.

"Oh my God, Cain. Did you do all that damage?" I asked. I was sure it wasn't possible, but I had to ask.

Cain chuckled. "I wish. God, I wish. Black eyes don't settle in that fast, and I hit him in the jaw. I'll leave you two to talk," he said before exiting the room, leaving Lennox and I to stare at each other in silence.

Lennox

I didn't plan to go to my dad's, but my mom's escapades were driving me crazy. I didn't expect to arrive and find Cain tongue-fucking Amelia. When I heard her moans, I thought she might be alone or with my father. The thought of her with my father disgusted me, so I was glad he was still on his solo honeymoon. For a second, I thought he returned early. Then, I saw Cain between her legs, and an intense desire sparked inside me. I fucked up my chances with them both and couldn't undo what I did. I wasn't sure I'd ever be able to make up for it, either.

If I hadn't fucked it up, I could've joined them.

Amelia and I were silent as I sat at the edge of her bed, confused about why my father had put her in the guest room—unless she requested it. He was married to the hottest girl in our town, but he was celebrating their honeymoon alone, and they weren't sleeping together. I was missing pieces of the puzzle.

"We need to take care of you," Amelia said, standing.

I shook my head. "No, princess. I want to feel the pain. I deserve it."

I spent the last week fighting her out of my system, taking punishment from anyone who would give it, and fighting back to quell my rage. I looked and felt like I had been hit by a bus. I knew I deserved it for what I did. I had to spend time away to think of how to atone for what I did—how to mend my broken relationships with the three people I loved. I fucked things up because I couldn't admit that I loved them.

"Sit down, Lennox James," she demanded when I tried to get up to stop her.

"Sure, Mommy," I teased, flashing a smile.

She rolled her eyes and left the room without her pants on. I stared at her underwear on the floor, remembering what I just walked in on. My cock grew in my pants, and I adjusted to hide it. Amelia needed to know I saw her as more than just a hole for my dick. She needed to know I saw her as a person and loved her. I had much to make up for, and we had much to discuss. I thought I did what I wanted. I thought I had completed my mission. I realized how wrong I was when she told me she was my fucking stepmom. Nothing could compare to that heart-wrenching moment.

She returned minutes later with a first aid kit in her hand. "Don't worry. I'll make it hurt," she said with a malicious grin.

She sat beside me on the bed, grabbing my arms and examining my hands. When she did, she exposed her freshly cut wrists to me. She pulled away fast, grabbing sports adhesive wrap from the kit and clearing her throat. "Let me bandage these and clean them. Then, we'll worry about getting an ice pack for your face. God, you look like a fucking wreck."

I chuckled, and then my eyes darkened, looking back at her arms. "What did you do, Amelia? Why? You have everything you wanted." I couldn't comprehend why she'd harm herself again. I knew she did in the past, but I thought she was better.

"Sure, Lennox. I have everything I wanted," she huffed, taking an alcohol wipe and pressing it hard against the open cuts on my knuckles. I winced in pain. She was right; she made it hurt. "You ruined my image at school. You made men think they could make disgusting advances at me. You destroyed my trust and my heart. And I had to marry my...I had to marry someone I didn't want to," she said quietly, looking away as she delivered the last line.

"You didn't have to marry anyone. You're an adult, and you made your decision. You married my dad. He will treat you the same as he treated my mother—the woman who loved you and let you in our house. Let you come to dinner with us," I said, bile running up my throat with each word. Thinking about her with him would drive me insane. My father was a piece of shit, and Amelia was a bargaining piece for him. When I fled last week, he had the biggest shit-eating grin. He loved delivering the blow about marrying my childhood best friend.

Amelia wanted to destroy me. With the help of my father, she did. She almost killed me, too.

"It's cute what you think you know, Lennox," she responded while wrapping my hand in the self-adhering wrap. I was no stranger to the kind she used. I fought people for money. It was often used in our line of sport. For days, I opted to hurt instead. She got up and threw on a pair of pajama shorts, leaving the underwear off. She climbed back into bed. "I'm going to bed now," she announced.

"You still owe me, or I'll tell my dad," I threatened. She might not have cared about him, but something was happening, and I felt she didn't want him to know about Cain. I could've taken advantage and had her let me touch her, but that wasn't how I wanted to win her over. I wouldn't touch her again until she begged for it.

She sighed. "And what do you want? A blowjob?" My cock twitched at the offer.

I climbed into bed behind her, wrapping my arms around her and pulling her body against mine. Once my father returned, this couldn't happen. I let my hand slide down to her hips, holding her body against mine.

"Mmm, tempting, but no. I want to cuddle. I want to hold you while I can," I told her. "I want to feel the warmth of your body against mine, knowing I almost died and lost it."

"The cuts aren't new, you know," she said. She lay frozen on her side, not moving an inch. She refused to melt into me like I wanted, and I couldn't blame her.

"I know every inch of your body, Amelia. Those cuts are new. Whatever happened, you can tell me."

She laughed. "I'm not telling you shit, Lennox. You don't deserve to know my story yet. You fucked up. When I reveal everything to you, I want it to destroy you. I want it to destroy you like it destroyed my mother. I watched her become a shell of a person like you watched yours. But your mother had a different reason for becoming who she is. You should ask her about it," she said bitterly. It took all my internal strength to hold back from fighting. My mother was innocent in this. She was cheated on, and she was raped for it. Then, her husband left her.

"Did you really stab your father?" I asked the question that had been on my mind for a week. I wasn't sure she'd give me a direct answer. When she remained quiet, I became certain she wouldn't.

She laughed. "I didn't make that up, Lennox. He's dead. He deserved it. He killed my mother when I was at school after he sent me to that horrible place. When I came back, I killed him, then I ran," she admitted. It took her becoming vulnerable to tell me. I could've told someone else. I could've turned her in. I wouldn't, but she risked it to tell me the truth.

"If you hated him enough to kill him, why'd you defend him that day, then ignore me when you moved? You moved before we could talk about it, and you broke me." There was so much more I wanted to talk to her about, but I didn't want to overwhelm her.

"Back then, I—he was my dad, Lennox. I was a scared, confused kid who looked up to her father. He wasn't always awful to me. And he always manipulated me into thinking everything was my fault," she explained. My fingers dug deeper into her hips until she winced, then I loosened my grip. I wasn't mad at her; I was angry *for* her. "And I didn't give up. I called you, and your mother told me never to call again. She said you didn't want to speak with me. She said you hated me. And I never got any letters from you." I always looked at my mother with love and adoration, but hearing Amelia say unexpected things about her, I wondered how innocent my mom truly was. I knew Amelia wasn't going to give me the answers I sought. And if she never got my letters, my mom never sent them, or her dad intercepted them.

"I'm sorry," I told her. She didn't respond, and I figured she was finally falling asleep again. She had an exhausting night. "He returns in a few days, and everything will change."

I played with her hair while lying behind her, inhaling the beautiful scent I've admired since we were kids. Her scent and warmth were what kept me calm and collected. Even when she fell asleep, I didn't move. I couldn't sleep, so I was there whenever she woke up screaming in a cold sweat. We had watched her for weeks, and she didn't react like that. It was breaking my heart to witness. I destroyed who she was to the point she was cutting herself and having nightmares, and all I could do was try to fix it while she remained married to my dad.

Amelia

The day came for Henry to return from Europe. A day I hadn't been looking forward to. We were finally signing paperwork to hold up his end of our deal—the part that would fuck over Lennox. Even if he was more tolerable, it needed to be done. He wasn't afraid to risk everything to get back at me, so I had to treat him the same.

I didn't know how I'd handle being in the house with him now. We avoided each other for the past several days because he had left and disappeared again before I woke up after falling asleep in his arms. Lennox, Cain, and Wolf didn't tell me where they were. Cain appeared out of nowhere, ate me out, and then disappeared with Wolf again. Maybe Lennox fucked off to join them.

I missed my home, even if it was tainted, knowing that Henry was the one who bought that house and gifted it to me under the pretense of a housing scholarship. He said it was mine to keep, and after a few weeks, I could go back occasionally. Our marriage was one of revenge and money, not one of love.

My heart sank when his office staff congratulated me. They didn't seem to think anything was off about Henry marrying an eighteen-year-old girl. They probably didn't know he knew me as a child, and they probably didn't know he didn't stop back then, either. Age was nothing to a man like him. He waited years to be able to marry me, he told me. I was disgusted by the notion, but I wanted my revenge more, and now I was paying for it.

Rather, Henry was.

But I got something out of it beyond revenge, too. Thanks to my sly, sneaky mother. She'd be a mix of proud of and disappointed in me. In the end, I'd make her proud. She believed in making men suffer for what they did, and there was no one she wanted to suffer more than Henry James. Henry didn't understand he wasn't buying my compliance; he was buying himself time. One month, legally.

"Hello?" I called out as I entered the home. It was quiet, but I was sure he got home hours ago. I looked around but saw no sign of Henry or Lennox. I headed upstairs to his office, where I heard two male voices inside—Henry and Lennox, I recognized. I gulped before knocking on the door.

"Come in," Henry called out. I entered the room, and Lennox looked like he was ready to leap from his chair and murder me. He sat opposite Henry, who was seated at his desk.

"I was just telling Lennox the news," Henry said smugly. I knew what he meant by the devious look on his face. He wanted nothing more than to rub everything in Lennox's face as much as possible. I wanted to, too, at the time, which was why I went with the conditions I set down.

"Oh?" I said, wanting to hear him say it.

"About how I'm making you the sole beneficiary to my will," he said. "It's already done, Amelia. No need to sign the paperwork. You're my wife." He winked at me.

I didn't want to go anywhere near him or let him lay a finger on me, but it felt fitting in the moment. I walked over to him, leaned down, and kissed him on the cheek. I put on a fake smile, gritting my teeth. "Yes, I am. All yours," I said. My eyes traveled to Lennox's hands, which were gripping the chair so tight it looked painful. I knew he, Cain, and Wolf told me I belonged to them, so I wanted to say I belonged to someone else.

"Can I leave now, father? I'd prefer not to see you and my stepmother right now," Lennox gritted out. I could tell his control was slipping. He had already been on edge, so I didn't know what he'd do.

"You may. We'll see you at school in a few days." I wanted to slap the smirk off Henry's face. At least with him, I didn't need to fake anything. We had a deal, and we knew what it entailed. For everyone else, I might need to pretend.

Lennox stomped out the door like a pissed-off teenager. I took his place in the chair.

"I have to hand it to you, Amelia. You were right when you said it'd piss him off. You know my son well. Probably better than me," Henry commended, chuckling.

Before Henry told me his plan, I thought he loved his son. I learned weeks ago that he's hated his son since his birth. He never wanted a child. It was part of why he resented his wife despite loving her. He turned on her quickly when she fell apart, and he told me he blamed me for what happened to her. Somehow, both he and Lennox blamed me. Henry's reasoning was worse.

"I've faxed the marriage license to your trust lawyer to show proof. It should be released to you soon. Until then, you're mine, Amelia," he told me. He stood up from the desk and walked toward me, leaning his ass on the desk and crossing his arms. His knees were too close to mine, and I felt like vomiting.

Being this close to Henry and a desk made me uncomfortable. It made it worse, knowing it was the same desk from when I was younger. "Which means, for my image and yours, you will not be seen fucking around with Cain, Wolf, or my son." His voice had a possessive tone, which I didn't like.

"Yes. I won't be seen with them for now," I said. I looked down, refusing to look him in the eye. I shifted in the seat, uncomfortable with the stare I felt coming from him.

He chuckled. "We're going to be married until I say otherwise, Amelia. Give up any notion that you have a chance with them because you're mine. You were owed to me. I will not see Cain back in this house." My eyes widened as I looked up at him and his smug smile. "Yes, I know he was here." How the hell did he know? I'd have to be careful moving forward. I wouldn't fuck up this deal. It would cost me too much at this point, including my soul.

"I'm sorry," I muttered bitterly. I wasn't, of course. We all know he was fucking his way through Europe days after marrying me. "Wait. I was owed to you? I remember that from the note, but you've never explained."

"Yes, Amelia. Your dad signed a contract. I never needed to show you because you easily agreed, but he signed you over to me." I blinked a few times, processing the information. Bile rose in my throat. He wasn't even my fucking father, and you can't legally sell a human being.

"I don't believe you," I said, though I did believe him. Mason Perkins would sell me like he sold me to the boarding school principal. Once he learned he could get money for me, he did what he could to get it. Apparently, including selling me to the neighbor—a fact he didn't get to tell me before I killed him.

Henry walked to his desk, opened a drawer, and handed me a

manila folder. I opened it to see a contract my dad had signed, stating I'd be eligible to marry Henry after turning sixteen. But when I was old enough, I was being passed around at school. Mason played him for money, and then we disappeared. But it didn't matter in the end because he tracked me down anyway, and I fell into his trap.

"If you don't let me leave you when my trust period ends, I'll…I'll tell the cops," I threatened, my voice mousy and unconvincing.

He broke out into a maniacal laughter. "Go ahead. Want to know who the Chief of Police is?" he asked, a brow cocked. "My poker buddy. I'll make sure to warn him about my new wife and her habit of lying. Or maybe I'll bring up a certain Nathan who mysteriously died near your work before you moved here," he said maliciously. I had never been more frustrated or helpless in my life. "And trust me, if you act out, I have ways to straighten your act up. I'm not the only man that'd pay to fuck you, and I happen to know men who would. They wouldn't be nice about it."

"Why would you want me anyway? You know my heart belongs to them; this was just an arrangement. I don't love you, and I never cold."

"I don't need your love. I need your submission, and I'll get it. You ruined my wife by telling your dad. He retaliated against Sabrina *before* I learned you could easily be bought. I was bad at showing it, but I loved her. I'm going to ruin you worse than Lennox ever could, and I'm going to keep you here until I'm done with you."

Henry leaned down, harshly gripping my jaw between his fingers and forcing my face to his. He kissed me roughly, but only for a few seconds. "How about you go make dinner, wife?"

I got up to leave, and he smacked my ass so hard I winced. I refused to turn around and show him. I didn't want to give him the satisfaction of knowing he hurt me.

"Sure. I will," I answered calmly, trying to keep him happy so I could remain alive and untouched as long as possible.

Lennox

When I left my house, I didn't know if I was more angry about Wolf and Cain hooking up or Amelia getting my inheritance. I was his child, while she had been his wife for five minutes. All I knew was my heart took me to the cabin. I had figured out they were staying there. It was a property we all found and owned together. I should've thought of it sooner, but my mind was stuck on Amelia marrying my father. I let my best friends fall to the side, mainly because they didn't want to see me, anyway. Now, it was time.

The motorcycle out front threw me off. None of us owned a bike, and no other cars were around. I walked toward the front door, opening it slightly before stepping in. There were lamps on inside, and I felt comfortable walking into a place I was the partial owner of.

"Cain? Wolf?" I called out, stepping inside. I could hear a television on, but I couldn't picture those two sitting around watching TV. But what else did they have to do up here?

"Lennox?" Wolf said, appearing in front of me with wide eyes. He had a bottle of Jack Daniels in his hand. When I looked around, Cain was sitting on the couch. He looked at me with hatred in his dark eyes.

"What are you doing here?" Cain asked.

He took a long drag of a cigarette, and I had never seen the man touch one before. He must've been really messed up. I felt fucking awful for that. I should've realized how much hurting Amelia would destroy Cain. He was obsessed with her—still is. I understood his obsession. I loved her when we were little, and I loved her now. I chose to ruin her instead of communicating. Maybe she had changed her mind about going for us. I'd never truly know because I didn't give her a chance to explain.

"Came to see my two best friends. Things went to shit at home," I said. While Cain sent me the video of Wolf and him, I hadn't spoken to them. They sent me into the situation with my father knowingly; they hinted so at the hospital.

"So, you found out Amelia is married to your dad?" Wolf said.

Cain looked pissed, but Wolf handed me the bottle he had been drinking from. I took a quick swig, then another, before handing it back to him. I sat next to Cain on the couch, with Wolf sitting in a neighboring chair. Cain looked at me with heated eyes before finishing his cigarette and heading to the kitchen. He came back with a beer in hand, giving it to me.

"Not only did I find that out when I left the hospital, after being stabbed, thank you, but I found out she's getting my inheritance. My dad cut me out of the will," I explained. I knew they wouldn't feel sorry for me, but I needed to talk about my problems for once. I didn't want things to build up until I exploded again. I wanted to show I could change.

"Do you even care about what happened between Wolf and I?" Cain asked, chuckling.

I scoffed, crossing my arms around my chest. "Of course, I care. Not in the way you want me to. I'm not angry. I have feelings for all three of you. It hurt to see you exclude me, but…I deserved it," I admitted. "If you two want to explore a connection, you should. But I won't stop wanting all of you, too. I'm going to fix it."

"Get him another drink," Cain ordered Wolf.

Their dynamic was strange. Between all of us, we were all dominant in one way or another. I had no idea how that would work out sexually, but I seemed to let Cain get control when it involved all of us. I let him tell Amelia and me what to do. I preferred to do the bossing around over getting bossed around, but when Cain did it, I didn't mind.

Wolf had no qualms about doing what Cain asked. He went into the kitchen area and grabbed a couple of shooters of Jack Daniels, handing one to me and keeping one to himself. We took a shot together, but Cain refused to drink.

"Do you want to prove you can fit into our relationship dynamic?" Cain asked, brow cocked.

"Yes," I said. My heart started to beat out of my chest as Cain leaned into me, his mouth centimeters from my ear.

"Suck my cock, Lennox. Let me fuck your face. You're so used to bringing girls to their knees; it's time someone brought you to yours."

My eyes widened.

"Fucking hell," Wolf muttered under his breath, groaning. Out of the corner of my eye, I saw him adjusting his erection and smirked. I loved knowing that Cain saying one sexual thing to me caused Wolf to be hard. I'd do whatever it took to earn everyone's trust back.

I stood from the couch and kneeled before Cain. Cain stood, smirking down at me. I took a deep breath and nervously fidgeted with the button on his pants before undoing it and pulling them down, along with his boxers. He was already hard and in my face. I had let Cain touch me, lick me, and blow me, but I had never been on the giving end.

The alcohol took away any doubts I might have had. I needed to do whatever it took to get things back to how they were. First, I needed the guys on my side. Then, I needed to reunite all of us with Amelia and get my dad out of the picture. This would be a good test of my limits in our abnormal relationship.

Cain budged his hips forward, his cock teasing my lips. I decided to open my lips and let him slip inside my mouth, the new taste hitting my taste buds but not making me want to gag yet. I opened my jaw wider to accommodate his girth, letting myself get used to the idea before bobbing my head slowly. I teased the head of his cock with my tongue.

Cain tangled his hands in my hair and made eye contact. "You know how to stop it," he said, reminding me of what we'd tell Amelia to do when we can't utter the safe word. I was determined, though. He ran his thumb along my cheek for a moment before he pushed himself deeper inside me, hitting the back of my throat. I surprised myself by not gagging. After he tested my gag reflex, he pulled out and then shoved himself inside harder. I tried to keep sucking his length as he pistoned his hips into my mouth, hitting the back of my throat each time. His hands firmly held onto my hair, and I grabbed his ass cheeks, squeezing.

I always thought I'd hate a dick in my mouth, but I didn't when it was Cain. I wanted to please him. I was a man who received many blowjobs, so I knew how. I did what I'd like to be done to me. I moved one hand to his balls, gently massaging them while listening to Cain's moans of pleasure. Hearing what I did to him made me moan against him, with his cock buried in my throat, sending the vibration through his length. He used my mouth rougher, forming tears in my eyes.

"Your tears are so pretty, Lennox," Cain cooed.

As someone who got off on humiliating people and watching them cry, it felt weird to be on the other end of it. But hearing Cain's praise encouraged me to work harder. I ran my tongue along the underside and head each time he pulled out.

"Christ, Lennox. I'm going to fucking come. If you don't want my cum down your throat, you better pull away now," Cain warned. I wasn't going to shy away from a challenge. I had a point to prove. I did the opposite. I took him deep in my mouth, so deep my throat constricted against the head of his cock, and gently pushed a finger into his ass. Cain exploded down my throat a second later, and I swallowed. Some of his come lingered around the corner of my lips. Before I could clean it up, Cain lifted me and brought me in for a deep kiss.

"I need another drink. And we have a lot to discuss, including what to do about Henry and whose fucking motorcycle that is outside." I walked to the kitchen and grabbed a few more beers for this conversation.

Cain laughed. "The motorcycle is mine. A gift I bought myself with my father's money. It'll make running for Levi easier, too." Cain grabbed a few helmets and handed one to me. "We're going to discuss what to do about Amelia and Henry, then I'm going to take your drunk ass home."

Amelia

I felt lucky knowing Henry didn't demand I sleep in the same bed as him. He told me he liked his privacy and would rather sleep alone. I discovered he had cameras in the halls so he'd know if Lennox or anyone went into my room. It was how he found out Cain visited. Even if he didn't know what happened, anyone could easily guess.

Though I was far enough from his room, I still felt too unnerved to sleep. Lennox hadn't returned, leaving me alone in the house with Henry. I locked my door to keep him away. The moment my eyes closed, I heard the rustling of a body falling through my window. My first thought was Cain—he loved to stalk me and show up while I slept, and he made it known. But as my eyes adjusted, I realized a drunk Lennox was on my floor, laughing.

"Lennox?" I questioned. I heard him giggling on the floor like a schoolgirl. I had never heard Lennox giggle. He was definitely drunk, if I couldn't already tell by the stench of whiskey in the room. "You smell like a distillery. You can't just disappear and reappear through my window, drunk as fuck at one in the morning." I rolled my eyes, but there was no way he could see.

Lennox stood up from the floor and dusted himself off before lying next to me. "Mm, I can, and I did." He wrapped an arm around my waist while I lay on my back, snuggling his face into my chest. It was unlike Lennox. Hours ago, he left during the meeting with his father. I couldn't believe he was here in my room. I didn't trust him. He couldn't forget his anger that easily.

"Why are you here, Lennox?" I asked. "And please say you didn't drive." I couldn't handle the thought of losing him in a car accident because of a stupid choice brought on by me. I knew he felt betrayed again. It was ironic that I cared, given what he did to me. I tried not to care, but my heart still hurt when I thought about him—when I thought about all of them.

He chuckled. "As if you'd care. But, no. I didn't. A sober Cain gave me a ride on his new motorcycle after he let me bitch and take shots for hours. Christ, Amelia. What the hell is going on? I know this isn't you. I know you don't belong to my father. I know you can't stand him. Do you really hate me that fucking much?" he asked, sounding pained. I sighed.

"Lennox, you destroyed me. Hell, you don't even care about me, so why are you here? I had to marry your dad, okay? It's complicated. Maybe I'll tell you one day if you earn that right. For now, I need you to stay away from me. If he catches us…" I said but was interrupted by Lennox.

"He'll *what?*"He sat up, looking at me. His eyes looked like a mix between angry and sad, and I felt terrible.

"Nothing. It's nothing. Henry wouldn't hurt me," I lied. I couldn't risk Lennox knowing any of the truth, except maybe about my trust. "You had just ruined me, and I needed help. Plus, I needed to be married to access the millions in my trust. Or reach twenty-one. I need to stay married for a time period, too. Or I lose it all and break my contract with Henry. So, you can't ruin my marriage," I explained, hoping it would hold him over for now.

"All this for money? You chose money and to hurt me over having a meaningful relationship?" He cocked a brow. It was ironic. I might have had different options if he hadn't released those videos to the entire school and made me a target for assault and ridicule. With my marriage to the dean, I was under his protection—for the most part. Most people had left me alone since returning, despite Lennox's public announcement to turn me into their personal whore.

"It's more than money, Lennox. I earned that money, but it was kept from me. My mother stole it for me, and she died for it. Then, my father found out and was able to put conditions on it before I took care of him. Since she was dead, he couldn't transfer the money to himself. He...wanted to marry me off to get me to access it. He planned to make me send it to him. I couldn't let it happen." My chest started to tighten when the memories began to flood my brain.

"I'm going to get you out of this mess, Amelia. I'm so fucking sorry for what I did. I should've realized my feelings for you sooner. I created this entire fucking mess, and I'm going to fix it," he said, shifting in the bed and moving toward my legs. He pried my thighs apart with his strong hands, settling between them.

"What are you doing, Lennox?" I asked, my breathing growing more rapid. Lennox never did anything without a motive or trying to get something in return.

He made direct eye contact while sliding my shorts off, exposing my bare pussy to the chill from the open window he hadn't closed. "Showing you how you're mine, no one can take you away. Especially not my father," he growled. Hearing me tell Henry I belonged to him sent Lennox into possessive overdrive. I wanted to fight him, but he stunned me into silence. He took my silence as his opportunity. He placed his arms under my thighs and pulled me toward him, burying his face in my pussy as he wrapped his cold lips around my clit, sucking.

I grabbed his hair with one hand, unsure if I was trying to push him away or pull him in as I tugged. My other hand gripped the bedsheet, pulling tight.

I squirmed beneath his mouth, but that only made him groan and suck my clit harder. Thankfully, his mouth started to warm up against my skin, though I didn't mind the sensation the cold brought. It was different. Tingly. Especially when the warm replaced the cold.

"Fuck, Lennox, that feels so good." My praise fueled him as he switched from sucking to flicking his tongue in circles slowly. "Oh, God. Don't stop. Please don't stop," I begged.

I felt a finger prodding my entrance and moaned at the contact. "You taste so good, Amelia. I'm sorry I've been missing out. I want to show you it's not just about me," he groaned. When he spoke, my clit missed the contact, and I bucked my hips up to bury in his face again. I could feel his grin before he took my clit more aggressively, his tongue moving side to side while he added a second finger. His fingers curled, hitting the glorious spot inside me that would send me over the edge soon.

Lennox's change in personality made me dizzy, or the impending orgasm did. I couldn't think straight when he was focused on making me feel good. It wasn't like him to give his full attention to pleasing someone else. He was fucking with my head. The only time he had eaten me out before, he was doing it as a psychological tactic.

All thoughts disappeared when he bit my clit before soothing it with his tongue. His mouth left my pussy. I groaned with disappointment. He watched my face with a smirk. My lips parted when his thumb replaced his mouth on my clit.

"I want to watch you come. I want to watch you fall apart from *my* touch," Lennox said, his eyes never leaving mine. He curled his fingers more, pushing them harder into me as I wiggled beneath him. His body pressed against mine so that I couldn't move. I tried to close my eyes so I wouldn't have to face him when he inevitably made me come, but he bit my nipple, and my eyes shot open. "Eyes on me, angel," he demanded.

My body obeyed. Lennox surprised me by leaning in and pressing his lips to mine in a searing kiss. I moaned into his mouth while his fingers worked magic. For someone who hardly took the time to focus on me, he was fantastic at it. His mouth swallowed all my moans while my tongue darted into his mouth, fighting with his. My hips leaped into the air while his lips left mine. I let out unintelligible curses, and Lennox grinned at me.

"Oh God, Lennox! Yes! That feels so good," I screamed, uncaring if anyone heard me at this point. I felt blissfully happy while my orgasm tore through me, turning my thighs into a shaking, quivering mess. He took my mouth in a kiss again, swallowing my screams until I calmed down. When we pulled apart again, I struggled to catch my breath. Once my shakes subsided, Lennox removed his fingers and lay on the bed beside me. He brought up the fingers that were inside me and sucked them clean in his mouth.

"You're so fucking beautiful when you come, Amelia," he cooed. I turned around to face the wall. He curled up behind me, pulling my body taut against his. "I don't give a shit if anyone catches us. You're mine, and I want you in my arms."

"Then why did you come in the window?" I teased.

I was so exhausted from my mind-blowing orgasm I didn't care that the window was open. I fell asleep in his warm embrace.

Cain

A few days ago, I dropped Lennox off drunk and resisted the urge to go inside the house and check up on Amelia. Lennox didn't live with his father, but he stayed with him, claiming he needed to while recovering. He was better, so it was clear he only did it to be around her. Amelia warned me it was dangerous after Henry told her about cameras around the house. It took a few days, but Wolf hacked into the camera's system. The ones they used weren't connected to his dad's security company. We were back in town now and ready to return to classes so I could follow her around again and ensure she was safe.

We couldn't act against her without knowing the exact terms of her trust inheritance; otherwise, we'd risk sabotaging her plan. We needed a solid plan against Henry, and she needed to help us now that we knew she didn't want him. Not that we would've accepted her being with Henry if she did want that. She was ours, regardless of blackmail. We knew she wanted us as well.

On days when Henry worked, and none of us had classes, we would have more time together.

Lennox told me he avoided the cameras by entering her bedroom window. Although it was late, I couldn't risk Henry being awake and monitoring the cameras. We could delete the footage later, and Wolf planned to loop the video he was working on, but for now, I had to borrow a page from Lennox's playbook. It was midnight when I entered through her unlocked window. Even in Lennox's home, Amelia still had poor security measures.

Amelia looked beautiful while she slept. The pale pink nightgown she wore was new. The way her nipples peeked through the light silk fabric made my cock start growing in my jeans. I missed watching her sleep. I didn't know how much until now. Fuck. I needed her badly.

I hurried out of my shirt, pants, and boxers, leaving them on the floor. I sat between her legs, hiking her nightgown up to give me access to her. She wore a cute pair of lace panties, and I felt a fury inside, wondering if she wore them for Henry. But if she wore them for Henry, she would've slept in his bed instead of alone. I tested how asleep she was by kissing the outer fabric of her panties, right over her clit. I pressed hard, and she didn't budge. My girl's a heavy sleeper.

Wolf liked to see her restrained, Lennox liked to see her cry, and I liked to see her face when I gave her pleasure she wasn't aware of—just as much as I liked to give her pleasure while she was awake, too.

I pulled her panties to the side and ran my tongue from her entrance to her clit before sucking her clit between my lips. I'd never get enough of her taste invading my mouth. Cute, soft whimpers left her mouth. I switched to licking slow, torturous circles, and she started to toss on the bed, her hips moving and pressing my face hard against her pussy. I didn't mind.

"Cain," she moaned. I halted, looking up at her, but her eyes were still closed. I smiled. Her body knew she was getting pleasured, and her mind filled in the pieces by telling her it was me. That's my girl. I rewarded her by licking down to her entrance and shoving my tongue deep inside, lapping up the juices that leaked because of me.

Her hips lifted off the bed, a soft moan leaving her parted lips. I replaced my tongue with my fingers, choosing to suck her clit into my mouth again, wanting to make her come quick. "Mmm, Cain, I love you," she mumbled words she never said while awake. I froze, removing my mouth and pulling down her panties.

I bit her thigh until she woke up, her eyes blinking as she looked down at me. "Cain?"

"It's me, Little Thorn. I came here because I need you so fucking bad," I admitted.

I moved up, hovering above her body and holding myself up with my palms.

"If Henry finds out you came here, he'll hurt you," she said in a sweet, groggy voice. She moved beneath me, trying to get away, but I put some of my weight on her to hold her in place.

"I don't give a fuck what Henry does. You're *mine*. He could hit me, beat me, stab me, or shoot me, and it wouldn't keep me away," I told her, reassuring her. She let Henry's threats keep us away from each other. I'd kill him for that alone, but he had other reasons to die, too. I couldn't help but blame myself, too. If I followed her from the game, she wouldn't have run into the arms of a manipulative psychopath. If she wanted revenge and money, I could've given her that.

I reached between us and ran my cock along her slit, gathering the wetness from her arousal and my tongue. Then, I nudged myself at her entrance until I was inside her. It was a quick, easy fit despite little foreplay. She moaned. My Little

41

Thorn was always ready for me. We fit together perfectly and easily because she belonged to me. Her body knew it, too. Her quiet, breathy moans told me she was enjoying it as much as I was, despite her being unaware she'd be having sex minutes ago.

"Being inside you is like being home," I said, peppering kisses down her jawline, neck, and collarbone. I stopped above the swell of her breasts, then took a nipple in my mouth, sucking and biting until her tiny body was writhing beneath mine. I could feel her struggle to remain quiet. She didn't want to get caught, while I didn't care if she woke the whole damn neighborhood. I sat up, placing my arms under her thighs and pulling her toward me, resting her legs on my shoulders. I slammed back inside her as she cried out, hitting her at a new angle I knew she liked.

"Fuck. Cain, I—," she moaned. I smirked.

"You what, baby?" I asked. I pushed my hips into hers, slowly but deeply, at a pace agonizing to both of us. Reaching down, my fingers roughly circled her sensitive, swollen clit.

"I love you," she blurted out, making me grin. She blushed when she realized what she admitted.

I pulled out, removing her legs from my shoulder and flipping her over so she was on her stomach. I grabbed her hips and pulled her up to her knees. "I'm obsessed with you, Amelia. There will never be another girl for me. I'm going to show you just how much I love you," I told her, grinning.

I lowered my mouth to her wet pussy, licking up her slit towards her cheeks. I spread her cheeks apart.

"You're not going to...lick back *there*, are you?" I couldn't help the laughter that escaped.

I answered her question by swirling my tongue around her

42

back entrance before plunging it inside, my fingers digging into her asscheeks. She buried her face into her pillow, moaning.

"Oh, God. That feels so good." Her fingers dug into the soft cotton, gripping as I feasted on her like she was my last meal. I never thought I'd eat a girl's ass, but I'd do anything for Amelia. "I want to feel you inside me…there," she said innocently.

"Where, Little Thorn?" I teased, pulling my mouth away and replacing it with a finger, plunging it in and out of her tight hole. She buried her face in the bedding and moaned.

"My ass, please," she pleaded. She didn't have to ask me twice. I had no issue using any hole available. I spit on her crack and let it drip down, adding another finger to loosen her up enough. She didn't have drugs this time. I worked her until a third finger fit, then pulled out and nudged my cock inside slowly, only feeding her an inch.

"How do you feel?" I asked, my hands pulling her cheeks apart to help push in.

"It hurts, but it's a good pain," she answered breathlessly, her fingers gripping the bedsheets as she raised her ass higher to me. "Fuck me, Cain. Don't hold back. I can handle it."

"You asked for it," I reminded her, smirking, before slamming inside of her and bottoming out. Feeling her tight ass around me was heavenly. "Fuuuuck, Amelia. I'll never get tired of this." I pulled out before slamming back in, setting a hefty pace that pushed her forward onto the bed. She was a moaning, sobbing mess beneath me. The sound of the headboard hitting the wall took over the room as she cried into the pillow.

I reached below and played with her clit roughly, her hips writhing beneath me at the pleasure. I held onto her hips with my free hand to still her while I watched her scream into the pillow as her orgasm hit her, her ass squeezing me while she fell apart.

"Do you want me to come in your ass, Little Thorn?" I was seconds away from coming as I plowed into her. I grabbed her hair into a pony and pulled her head back, pressing her back to my chest and hitting her at a new angle.

"Yes. Please come in my ass, *please*," she begged.

It didn't take long for my body to give in to her command. I stilled deep inside her, feeling my cum fill her. I kissed her neck while catching my breath before pulling away slowly and watching as my cum dripped out of her ass.

"A beautiful fucking sight," I whispered into her ear. "Stay here."

I went into her bathroom and wet a towel with warm water, bringing it to her and cleaning her off as she lay on her stomach. Then, I flipped her over and grabbed the small box from my pants pocket on the floor. "I got you something," I told her.

"Cain, that better not be a ring," she responded with a glare.

I smiled. "I'd rather tattoo my name on your finger than give you a ring that can be lost or replaced. Then, I'm stuck on you forever. No, this isn't a ring, baby girl. Open it."

I watched her eyes widen when she looked inside the box. Inside was a small necklace with a vial of my blood.

"What is this?" she asked, holding up the jewelry for inspection.

"My blood. You own all of me, Amelia. Including my blood, my heart, and my soul."

"You're crazy and psychotic, Cain. And I'm glad."

Cain grabbed the arm that held my cuts. I tried to pull it away, but it was like he knew what to look for. Did Lennox tell him what I did? Cain kissed the red, inflamed marks on my skin. "Only I'm allowed to make you bleed, Amelia. Remember that. If you feel like hurting yourself, if you feel like cutting, tell me, and I'll make you bleed."

Amelia

I wondered if I'd see Wolf, Lennox, or Cain on campus. Beyond seeing Lennox around the house when he appeared, I hadn't heard much from them. He hadn't bothered to sneak into my room again, nor did the other guys. When they weren't frantically apologizing in texts, I wondered if I somehow lost them. I shouldn't have cared. They treated me like garbage. Except, I forgave Cain and Wolf immediately, and my heart was warming up to the idea of forgiving Lennox. He was showing a different side to him, one that I could stand by and support. He had to show a lot more of himself for me to forget what he put me through, though.

It didn't stop me from falling for him. Sometimes, when I looked at Lennox, I saw my childhood best friend instead of the vicious, heartless monster he became.

The first person I saw on campus was Lily. She waited outside, running up to me before I could enter the door. Her face was stuck between a smile and a worried expression.

"I have been so worried since the game! I haven't been able to get ahold of you. Lennox hasn't been at school, either. What the hell is going on?" Lily questioned, squeezing my shoulders and shaking me. "I thought you killed them, then yourself."

I laughed at her insinuation. "They aren't worth it." I

46

shrugged. "I don't know where Wolf, Lennox, and Cain have been, but I've been settling in my new home," I answered without thinking. I didn't mean to give away my news so easily, but now I couldn't return.

"New home?" she questioned, cocking her head.

"In my house. But not with me, with my dad," Lennox interrupted. Lily's wide eyes looked toward me. "And what my dear Amelia means to say is she doesn't want to kill us. Then she wouldn't get such good di—"

I slapped a hand over his mouth. "That's enough, Lennox. My best friend was talking to me, not you." I rolled my eyes. Lily giggled. Lennox shrugged.

"I'm curious why you're even talking to him after what he did," Lily said, her arms folded across her chest as she looked Lennox up and down. "I should hurt you for what you did to her." The threat sounded adorable coming from her. Lily wouldn't hurt any living thing—not even a bug.

The campus started filling up with people, some stopping to stare at Lennox and me. Most of them were likely at the game where the videos and photos were shared, along with the message to treat me like a slut.

"Beg for me to forgive you, Lennox. Tell everyone gathering how you're fucking sorry," I commanded. "I told you I'd make you beg on your knees."

Watching Lennox's eyes widen was satisfying—a smirk formed on my lips.

"You want me to…what?" he questioned, cocking his head to the side.

"Beg me, Lennox James. On. Your. Knees." I repeated. It would be a test to see if he could set his pride aside and show me and everyone that he genuinely cared about me. I was sure he wouldn't go through with it. Lennox James wouldn't dare appear weak in front of a crowd.

"Fine," he said through gritted teeth. To my surprise, and everyone's, he knelt before me. "I want everyone to know that you're my girl, Amelia. I'm in love with you. I fucked up because I don't know how to love. You're not a slut, you're not anyone's toy but mine. No one can touch you." He looked around while yelling his apology, making sure people heard his decree about touching me. "Please, forgive me for being an idiot. I don't deserve you, but I need you. I'll fucking hurt anyone who touches you." He grabbed my hand and brought it to his lips, kissing my hand. "I'm unworthy," he said quietly, only for me to hear.

I backed up a few steps, putting distance between us. "Crawl to me," I challenged, crossing my arms on my chest. He looked at me with wide, apologetic eyes before inching toward me on his knees. He winced each time his knee smacked into the ground.

"Kiss my toes," I said, grinning at him. His jaw clenched before he leaned down and kissed my feet through my open-toed sandals. I giggled. "Okay, you can get up."

"Get fucking moving," Lennox shouted at the gathering crowd, looking around with a hard stare. They started to disperse, whispering their gossip.

"Aren't you scared word will get around to Daddy?" I teased.

"I hope it does," he responded in a low growl.

It was easy for Lennox to say that. He didn't threaten Lennox's life; he threatened mine.

Lennox placed a hand on my lower back, pulling me toward him and kissing me softly. "I meant every word I said," he whispered against my lips. I felt my heart leap and the corner of my lips tug into a smile.

"Get to class. I'm going to walk with Lily," I instructed. "I'll see you later." Lennox obliged, walking away. He'd do almost anything I asked while trying to get back into my good graces.

I turned to face a jaw-dropped Lily. "What did I miss?" she asked.

"I married Lennox's dad when I was pissed and needed help. He got the cops off my back, and now I get access to my inheritance and money he paid me to marry him, too," I explained. Lily was sweet and innocent, but she was my friend, and I trusted her. I knew she'd support any decision I made. Hell, she'd support me if I had killed Lennox in front of her moments ago.

"Wow. That's...a lot. Let me walk you to class, and you can explain in more detail."

***

I felt thankful when my last class of the day ended, and Lily acted no different toward me in class. She proved herself to be a real friend when I needed one. Throughout the day, I had things thrown at me, rude comments made, and someone spat on my lunch food. Lennox's decree didn't reach the entire campus yet, and some still felt like they could fuck with me.

The best part of the day was knowing the professor I fucked with was gone and replaced by someone else. I didn't feel bad. It would be easier on me knowing I wouldn't have to see him now. I'm sure Henry fired him when we got married. My escapades with him were broadcast to everyone. He was a liability now.

"Are you sure you're okay leaving alone?" Lily asked, frowning. I nodded, and she walked off. I planned to stay on campus and study. Even if Henry was also here, being in his house felt weird. I wanted Lily to leave because I wanted to be alone. I

49

didn't get far, though.

Cain found me outside the library. He grabbed my hand and ushered me into the darkness of the stairway. He used his body to press me against a wall, smiling down at me. "I've been looking for you." I felt his cock hardening against my stomach as he leaned in and kissed along my jawline and neck. I moaned, feeling myself melting against the wall until Cain grounded me by grabbing my hips.

"Cain, we can't do this here," I whispered.

"No one can see us, Little Thorn," he responded.

He kissed me hard, our lips coming together sloppily and one of his hands gripping my hair. His tongue fought against my lips for entrance, and I let him in, battling inside my mouth. I reached a hand into his hair, gripping a few strands tightly as I pressed my lower body into his.

He pulled away breathlessly. "As much as I want this, I came here to grab you and bring you somewhere," he said, his forehead resting against mine. I groaned. "If you make noises like that, though, I'll have to tell Wolf to fuck off while I keep you to myself."

"I'm going to see Wolf?" I questioned. I hadn't seen him since the game, and my heart pattered at the thought. Since it had been weeks, I thought he had lost interest in me.

Cain grinned. "I'm supposed to take you to him right now."

He pushed away from the wall, taking my hand in his and walking us out of the staircase and into the parking lot. He brought us to a parked motorcycle, and I froze, looking up at his smiling face. "We're not going on that thing, are we?" I asked.

He reached into a bag, grabbed a black helmet, and handed it to me. "Yes, we are. Hot, right?" He winked before putting his helmet on.

He sat on the bike and then patted the seat behind him. "I promise you'll be safe," he said.

"If you kill me, I'll haunt you," I replied, climbing on the backseat and wrapping my arms around his waist.

"If I kill you, I'll kill myself and spend eternity with you." Most women would be put off by men saying something like that, but Cain was my brand of crazy.

Amelia

C ain dropped me off at a cabin half an hour from town, and I wondered if this was where he and Wolf were hiding out before. It seemed cozy but was mostly dark, sending my anxiety into high drive. He wouldn't send me to be killed, would he? I opened the front door. Candles and a few dim lamps mostly illuminated the room. It almost seemed... romantic until my eyes landed on the bed in the middle of the room.

"Wolf. What is this?" I asked, staring in disbelief at a tied-up, naked Wolf. His arms were tied with rope and connected to metal hooks on the wall. His ankles were tightly linked to the end of the bed, leaving him little wiggle room. It looked uncomfortable and very similar to the position he had left me in before. The Wolf I knew would've never willingly been like this. He thrived on control; he needed it to let anyone close to him.

"I had Cain leave me like this for you. Fuck, Amelia. I need you to know I belong to you as much as you belong to us. Take advantage of me. Hurt me how I hurt you that night when I tied you up and left you there. I can take anything you give." He looked sincere as we locked eyes while I stayed across the room, unable to take a step yet. There were toys at the end of the bed. A paddle, a beaded dildo, lube, and a few more things I had never seen before.

"You can use any of the toys. I can handle it. If I can't, I'll use the safe word.'" We kept the same safe word no matter who was using it. All of us wanted to be safe and stop things if needed. It mattered to Cain and I because of what we went through. No one wanted to push boundaries, especially when Cain and Wolf were developing a new relationship.

After looking at the toys, I knew what I wanted to use. I needed to release anger and have fun, and Wolf offered himself up to me. I'd eagerly give him what he wanted. I walked toward the bed, looking at the toys before undressing myself. I wanted to match Wolf, and he was completely naked.

"Fuuuck," Wolf said as he watched me shed my clothes. "I've missed your body," he mumbled. "I fucking need you," he groaned. I picked up my toy of choice and joined him in the bed, settling between his legs. Wolf looked at the toy with wide eyes, smirking. "Mmm, that's new, Little Lamb."

I wasn't used to being in control. I didn't mind letting the men take control, but Wolf offering himself up meant a lot to both of us. I knew it was hard for him. He wouldn't pick out the toys if he didn't want them.

"I want to make you feel good," I said. I ran my fingers down his chest, stopping before the V in his lower abdomen. They were all so fucking hot, but Wolf had the most toned body. He was a beautiful sight with his wild blonde curls. I teased his nipples, and his mouth parted, the expression on his face awakening excitement in me. I leaned forward, bringing Wolf's nipple into my mouth and swirling my tongue around it. I looked at him through my lashes, watching him bite his lip.

"Your tongue feels amazing," he whispered. "I didn't think

I'd enjoy that so much." I bit his nipple lightly, then sucked. His hips moved beneath me, his cock seeking friction. I moved away to tease him, pulling my body from his and sitting between his thighs again without touching him anywhere. I wanted to torture him a little. Wolf was into orgasm denial, and it was his turn to suffer a little.

I grabbed the small bottle of lube I brought onto the bed and squirted some into my hand. Wolf wiggled his brow as he watched me lube the dildo, but I didn't bring it to him, instead slowly inserting it into my pussy.

"Christ, Amelia. You're going to kill me," he said breathily. I moved the toy in and out a few times before removing it. I lined up the slick dildo at Wolf's hole, watching as he took a deep breath. His eyes closed in preparation, and I inserted the dildo inside, moving slowly, inch by inch, until it was mostly inside him. I watched his ass swallow the toy with fascination. I never thought I'd be into it before, but I was.

"Fuck, Wolf. That looks so good," I said, lips parted while I watched. I angled the toy upward, not knowing much about male anatomy, but I must've hit something because Wolf started to struggle in the rope, his body writhing.

"Ffuuuucck. Oh God. It—it feels so fucking good. I've never done this before." Wolf threw his head back.

I leaned forward, wrapping my lips around the swollen, pink head of his cock. His beautiful, glorious cock. I flattened my tongue and ran it along the underside before sucking the head into my mouth again. I never thought I'd missed giving blow jobs, but now that I had control over it, I did.

Unable to do anything else, Wolf's hips lifted off the bed, sending him further into my throat. I moaned around the length. Cain was the thickest, and Wolf was the longest. It didn't take much for him to hit the back of my throat. I gagged while I adjusted, and then I let him rest in my throat, swallowing to tighten my throat around him. His body jerked at the sensation, and I knew I was doing good. When I pulled back, his cock and the corner of my lips were covered in spit. I swallowed his cock whole again, swirling my tongue around his length while he was deep in my throat. The only sounds filling the room were my slurping and his moaning. The sounds that came from him made me want to keep going. He was a moaning, whimpering mess.

I reached between us and started to rub his balls in my hands, wanting nothing more than to make Wolf feel good and feel in control. Once his hips started rapidly pounding into my face and his breathing increased, I pulled away, leaving him reeling.

"I was about to come. Fuck," he said. I smirked down at him.

"I know. I can't have that yet. I'm not ready for you to come. I want you to come when you're inside me, Wolf," I explained.

"I need to be inside you now," he responded, groaning.

"Beg," I told him. His arms struggled in the ropes, his head falling back with a groan.

"Please, Little Lamb. Please fuck me. I want to come inside you. I've never needed anyone more." He sounded breathless at the end of his pleas.

I would've settled for one word, but he gave me more. I moved up, hovering above him with my knees on either side of his legs. I reached down to grab his already slick cock, lining him up with my entrance and slowly lowering myself down until he was sheathed inside me. I took a moment to adjust to his size before beginning to move my hips again. I wasn't used to being in control, but I liked it. I propped myself up by clawing at his chest, digging my nails into the skin until I drew blood.

"Oh fuuuuck, Wolf. I missed this so much," I told him, my breathing picking up as I started moving my hips up and down. I angled myself more to take him in deeper, moaning each time our hips met.

"Oh, shit. Amelia. I can't last. You feel so fucking good, baby," he said. "No one will ever compare. I fucking need you."

I leaned in, burying my face in his neck and taking in his scent. Then, I bit into the skin and started to suck. I wanted to mark his skin with my marks, showing he belonged to me like I belonged to them. He moaned while I left marks on his neck before trailing my lips down his chest, taking a nipple into my mouth and sucking.

"Your lips feel so good on my skin," he praised, his hips thrusting harder into mine. I moaned loudly against his skin. Then, I bit down on his nipple until he started to thrash. "Christ, Amelia. I'd punish you if I weren't the one tied up," he said, his eyes darkened as he looked at me. I grinned.

"That's what you get for what you did to me, Wolf. I shouldn't even reward you by letting you come inside me, but I need it so bad. I need to feel you fill me up again. Show me you own me." I flattened myself against his body before moving my hips again, my clit rubbing against his pelvis with each thrust. I felt the orgasm blooming in my core and moved my hips quicker and harder to let it build faster. "Oh, fuck, Wolf. I'm going to come." I moaned, my hand reaching up and tugging on his hair. I had never been so aggressive or in control before, and I liked it because Wolf was the dominant and controlling one. It made me feel powerful.

"Mmm, come all over my cock, baby," Wolf demanded.

My body listened, my walls tightly clenching him in waves

while my orgasm began to quest. Wolf threw his head back, his moans growing more erratic as he stilled. I pushed myself down, making sure all of him was inside of me. He came with a loud grunt, his body trembling beneath me. The moment was blissful. I collapsed at his side, watching his chest rise and fall as the sound of our heavy breathing took over the room.

I stood up a minute later, threw on my clothes, and walked toward the door to leave.

"Wait, Amelia! Aren't you going to let me out?" Wolf questioned, looking at me with wide eyes.

I smirked. "No, Wolf. I'm sure Lennox or Cain will." I walked back to him, leaning down and gently kissing his lips. "Consider it a punishment or a lesson, babydoll," I taunted before stepping away.

"RED! RED!" he yelled, despite me not being far from the bed. I turned to see a panicked look in his eyes, like he was seconds from a mental breakdown. His body was thrashing in the restraints. I hurriedly untied him from the rope holding his ankles and arms and jumped on the bed to bring him into my arms as he curled into himself.

"I'm so sorry, Wolf. Talk to me. What happened there?" I asked. I leaned over to the bedside table and grabbed the bottle of water that someone placed there, handing it to him. He didn't react, didn't move. He stared at the wall. I felt my heart breaking for him. It took a lot for him to open up to me the way he did, and I ruined it somehow. I snuggled behind and pulled him to my chest, playing with his hair while he lay there. It took him several minutes, but he finally broke the silence.

"I need to be in control because I lost it when I was thirteen. My mom had her high school friend watch me sometimes. And one day, she decided to tie me up to the bed and take my virginity. I had barely been able to get a boner back then. Since I did, she said it was clear I wanted it. I couldn't do anything. I was small, weak, and tied up. I vowed never to be so weak again. I vowed never to feel like I wasn't in control again. I'm really, really sorry for what I did to you that night. I need you to know that I'm in love with you, Amelia."

My heart broke with every word he said; then he pieced it together again with his confession. "You were a kid, Wolf. Your body reacted in a normal way. It doesn't mean you wanted it. That's still rape," I told him.

"She told me it's not because I wanted it. I believed her. I tried to tell someone, but they said I was a guy and I should feel lucky that it happened to me. What you and Cain went through is something much worse."

"No, Wolf. Neither is worse. We all went through something awful in our own way. Don't listen to anyone telling you otherwise, okay? Cain, Lennox, and I love you. Only listen to us." I peppered kisses along the back of his neck. "I'm going to tell you something no one else knows. Henry is the one who took my virginity when I was twelve."

Wolf

I thought telling Amelia the truth the other night was the hardest thing I had to do. It turns out that heading to campus and knowing the truth about Henry was harder. Amelia asked me not to tell anyone what she said and said I couldn't make it obvious to Henry. We'd both be at risk if he found out. Amelia needed to do whatever she needed to exact revenge on Henry; then, she'd be with us.

I had been back at my dad's place since Cain and I had decided to leave the cabin. Soon, we'd have to face Lennox again, and I wasn't sure how I'd lie to his face about his dad and keep my emotions calm. I had to figure it out. If I betrayed her trust, she'd betray mine. She knew my secret now. Something only Cain and Lennox knew. It might've been crazy for me to trust her after what she did, but I knew she did what she thought she needed to. I wouldn't have been in that position if it hadn't been for Lennox dragging me into his plan, and I could only blame myself.

When my eyes first landed on Amelia, I noticed her breath hitched when we made eye contact. I stopped in my tracks. After the other night, everything felt more intimate between us. I clenched my fists at my sides, remembering the way I was tied up and how she made me feel like I had power even when

I had none.

I never expected to fall for anyone, but especially not her and Cain. I loved them both, and they had similar traumas. They understood my trauma and loved me still. I felt lucky, even with the confusing situation with Lennox. Amelia didn't tell me, but I knew they fucked around at his dad's place—which was now her place. Thinking about her marriage to Henry made me physically ill. She hadn't mentioned why she married him entirely, but I always knew there was something more to it.

Amelia walked toward me, and my body tensed. I was happy to see her but nervous to be around her. I wasn't the one who was public with her like Cain and Lennox were. Affection wasn't my thing. Would she expect it now?

"Hey, Wolf," Amelia said, batting her eyelashes as she approached. "I have something I want to show you," she said. She took my hand, causing a fluttering in my stomach, and led me away from the groups of people walking around campus. She brought me to a bathroom down the hall—the bathroom where I initially saw her on her knees for Lennox. Cain and Lennox were in the bathroom, surprising me.

Lennox smirked at me before leaving the bathroom. I wasn't sure why.

"It's hard for us to find alone time with Henry back. Lennox will watch the door and prove he can be a team player. Cain and I...we want to share you. If you'll let us," Amelia offered, sinking to her knees before me. Cain joined her on the hard tile floor. I looked down at them with wide eyes, frantically nodding my head. I never wanted anything more than I wanted them in that moment. Weeks ago, I never even imagined Cain would be involved.

"Oh, thank fuck," Amelia responded before undoing my belt and unbuttoning my pants, pulling them down to my ankles. Cain went in and pulled down my boxers, my already hard cock springing free in his face.

"Christ, I forgot how fucking big it is," Cain groaned.

"I want to watch you first," Amelia said, her voice full of lust. She loved the idea of Cain and I together. She'd watch any of us together if she could. She was our dirty, needy girl. Ours to love, fuck, kiss, and share.

Cain wasted no time pleasing Amelia and me by wrapping his pretty lips around my thick cock, his tongue working on my head, licking at the precum that started leaking when I saw them on their knees for me. It was a beautiful yet surprising sight.

"Jesus, Cain," I groaned, leaning back against the wall with my body and palms to support my weight. Amelia grinned. Cain was good at what he did. Of course, he was. He and Amelia had the same fucked up experience. It made me mad to remember why they were so good at sucking cock, but they were mine now. They'd only touch me and Lennox for the rest of their lives. No one would hurt them again.

Amelia placed kisses along my thigh while Cain took me deep in his throat, swallowing the head of my cock down his throat, his tight, wet heat engulfing me and sending a tingle up my spine. Cain swirled his tongue around my leaking slit, licking up my precum that continued to drip. Amelia started to bite into my skin, then lick over the area to soothe where she'd bite. Their movements together were driving me so insane that I wasn't sure I'd last very long.

"My turn," Amelia said. Cain pulled away, and I groaned from the loss, but it was quickly replaced by a moan of pleasure when Amelia took me to the back of her throat seconds later, her tongue swirling around the underside of my cock at the same time. Cain's hands roamed my body, his fingers landing on my nipples and pinching. I threw my head back against the wall.

I reached a hand forward and entangled it in Amelia's hair, holding her nose to my pelvis as I listened to her gagging on my cock. The sound turned me on like no other. I loved listening to her struggle. I loved the way mascara ran down her face when she struggled. The way she sounded when she pulled off and gasped for air.

Cain's hand moved between my cheeks, rubbing at my puckered hole lightly. It sent further into Amelia's throat before I pulled my hips back, giving her space to breathe again. She pulled her mouth off me. Cain and Amelia both took a side of my cock, licking, kissing, and teasing. Cain's finger breached the tight ring of muscle and curved to rub against my prostate.

"Oh fuck," I moaned. "Who is going to take my cum?" My breathing was becoming heavier, and my balls were tight and ready to blow. If someone did wrap their mouth around my cock fully, I was going to blow all over them. We still had classes to attend, so I figured they didn't want that.

"Me," Cain said. Amelia removed her mouth, and Cain sucked me into the back of his throat, his finger working me harder in my ass until I came with a loud grunt, trying to keep my noises down. I leaned against the wall, catching up on my breathing.

"God, I don't know what I did to deserve you guys," I told them.

"Let's go, we've got class," Lennox said, popping his head in the doorway.

***

I didn't tell anyone I planned to see my dad for dinner. We didn't talk much. He wasn't the emotional type. He was focused on his security business and had dozens of employees to take care of, and as he would say, security didn't rest. He was in charge of things like providing business and residential security officers, setting up security systems, and private security if needed. I helped him with the technical side sometimes. He wasn't a bad dad unlike Lennox, Cain, and Amelia's dads.

I enjoyed his company but couldn't look him in the eye. This dinner was about being open. If I could be open with Amelia about my past, I could be with him, too. He deserved to know the truth.

"Wolf! I was surprised when you invited me to dinner," he said, sitting across from me. I handed him a menu, but I wasn't sure I could sit through a full dinner. The nerves made me nauseous.

"I needed to tell you something," I told him, my eyes focused on the menu.

"You can tell me anything, Wolf. You're my son, and I love you," he said. He made me feel at home no matter where we were. I appreciated his words, which made me feel more at ease with what I was about to say. I was about to change his life almost as much as it changed mine.

The waiter stopped to take our drink orders. Dad ordered a water, and I ordered a Coke. We ordered Mozzarella sticks as an appetizer—our regular deal. I used the time our waiter was gone to tell Dad. I was less of a flight risk if I had mozzarella sticks waiting for me. I needed to tell him now or never. Amelia made me feel empowered, but that wouldn't last long.

"Dad, when I was thirteen...my babysitter, Mom's friend...we had sex. I didn't understand what was happening. I—I'm sorry,"

I admitted. My heart started to race, sweat gathering on my forehead and palms. His face changed to confusion.

"What are you sorry for? Son, she raped you. We trusted Brittany in our house, and she took advantage of *my child?* Why am I just now learning about this?" I could tell from the rise in his tone that he was angry, but not at me.

"It gets worse…" I said, biting my lip. We were interrupted by the waiter dropping off our drinks and appetizer.

"Thank you, Jake. We'll need another minute to order," my dad said.

"How can it get worse?" he questioned.

"I told Mom. She said I should be lucky that an older woman like her wanted me." When I admitted what I told no one else in the world, I looked down at the table. Then, I ate a mozzarella stick while he processed it.

My dad slammed a one-hundred-dollar bill on the table and stood up. For a moment, I thought he was mad at me for ruining his life with that news. "I'll call you later. I'm going to take care of this." He started to walk away, but then he stopped, kissed me on the head, and left, leaving me there wondering what he would do.

I had a pretty good idea.

One that was confirmed when he called me later and told me my mother had succumbed to her illness after spending months on a home healthcare plan in his home.

Lennox

I never thought I'd be nervous for Cain to come over. My mom ran off with some prick, so the house was back to being mine for the time being. Cain and I agreed we wanted to spend time alone together. We wanted to explore our separate relationship while still being with Amelia. I wanted to know what it was like to lose myself to Cain without anyone watching. Could I relinquish control to him? Or would he relinquish to me?

The idea made me hard, and he'd be here any moment. I didn't have to impress my best friend, but part of me wanted to. I made chocolate-covered strawberries—Cain's favorite—and lit some fucking candles all over the place while dimming the lights. It wasn't like I ever had romantic sex, so I wasn't sure why I went for a hint of romance. Cain and I were dominants. We didn't need romantic shit. But I know what he went through with men in the past. I'd be the first guy willingly fucking him or being fucked by him. The honor meant a lot to me. I was ready.

I re-checked the area to make sure the lubes and condoms were on the living room table. I wouldn't be able to make it to the room once he entered through the door. But there were more upstairs, just in case. I didn't want to search around the house when we needed them.

I heard my phone ding from the kitchen counter and walked toward it, unsure what to expect. Of course, it was a text from Cain.

Go to your room. I have a surprise waiting for you.

Jesus Christ, he would find a way to sneak in and leave something for me. When was he here? How did he get in? I left my phone on the counter and hurried up the stairs and to my bedroom. Even when my mom was home, the master bedroom was mine. It was spacious, nice, and dark, like my soul. Just the way I wanted it. It kept her away. She said it gave her bad energy whenever she tried to take over the room again, and it wasn't like she had the energy to remodel.

My bedroom door was cracked despite knowing I had closed it this morning. I opened it slowly, unsure what to expect on the other side. It certainly wasn't a smirking Cain, but there he was, shirtless, hot as fuck, and currently, *all mine.*

"Are you going to stand there gawking, or are you going to make a move?" Cain teased, repeating our earlier conversation when Amelia first returned to Northridge. He sprung into action before I could answer—physically or with my voice. He stalked toward me, pinned me against the wall, and held me there with his hips. His erection rubbed against mine, and I groaned. I was happy that I could enjoy the feeling of cock and pussy. I had everything a man could ever dream of at my fingertips.

His lips pressed to mine roughly as my hips rubbed against his, seeking the friction of our cocks touching. I moved like a horny little bitch, moaning into his mouth as we both grew impossibly hard while rubbing together. He stole my breath away, our tongues fighting each other hungrily. Kissing Cain was very different from kissing Amelia. His stubble felt odd on my face, yet so good. I reached between us and unbuckled his belt, pulling it off and unbuttoning his pants, taking his boxers along with them, all without breaking our rough, passionate kiss. I let him think he had the upper hand as his hand gripped my throat, his teeth taking my bottom lip and biting until blood flowed into my mouth. Then, he licked it up and smiled against my lips.

When he pulled away, I struck. I pushed us until the back of his knees hit my bed, sending him flat on his back. He lifted himself by the elbows, looking down at me, his chest rising and falling in deep breaths. "Come get me, baby," Cain said, winking.

I hurried my pants off and left them on the floor with my boxers before jumping on the bed, placing myself between Cain's legs, his beautiful, swollen cock now in my face. I felt drool in the corner of my lips as I stared. I tasted him once before and wanted it now more than ever. I wanted to fuck him, too. I couldn't take too much time worshiping his cock like he deserved because I needed to be inside of him. I swallowed him to the back of my throat in one motion, sending his hips bucking up as my throat struggled. I gagged around his length and pulled back, already leaving a sloppy, slobbery mess on his cock. I pulled out to leave just the tip in my mouth, swirling my tongue slowly around the head and licking the precum from his leaking slit. I loved the salty, musky taste of Cain. It was a stark contrast to the taste of Amelia, but both were my favorite snacks.

"*Jesus*, Lennox," Cain groaned, his fingers intertwining in my hair and gripping harshly. "Take it slower. I don't want to blow my load before you're inside me."

Instead of taking him to the back of my throat again, I only went about halfway before withdrawing, sucking and slurping my way around his cock. But it wasn't his cock I needed to prep. While Cain was moaning and groaning from my mouth, I slipped a finger between his cheeks and prodded the tight ring of muscle slowly and gently with my finger. The sound of his moans filled the room, causing my hips to rut into the mattress, needing the friction.

"Look at you, sucking my cock but so fucking needy you're humping the mattress," Cain cooed.

I groaned around his length, causing him to grip my hair tighter and wrap a fist around the comforter we were lying on. Tired of him topping me from the bottom, I prodded a finger inside him. His hips bucked again, shoving his length down my throat, and I swallowed around him. "Oh fuck, baby. I need you to stop and fuck me," Cain begged. I pulled off his dick and smiled, satisfied with retaking control.

"I need to prep you so I don't hurt you," I told him. I added another finger, working them inside him to help loosen him up enough to take me. I needed to feel his ass clench around me *now*.

Cain shook his head. "No. I want it rough, please." Fuck. I knew about Cain's past and how he had been used, but I didn't know this side of him. Before Amelia showed up in our lives, he was a virgin who had only watched us before. And he didn't even get hard while watching us. Not until Amelia was involved, and I didn't blame him. Beyond him, no one really did it for me anyway.

I pulled out my fingers, determined to give Cain what he asked for. I needed to be who he needed me to be, and being rough was easy for me; I just never thought I'd be fucking Cain roughly. I wanted to be good enough for him.

"Flip over, Cain," I directed, moving away from his legs to give him space. "On all fours for me so I can see your pretty little hole."

Cain groaned and moved from his back to position himself on his elbows and knees, exposing himself to me. It was a beautiful sight. The way he and Amelia both submitted to me made me wonder what I did to get so fucking lucky to have both of them love me.

I ran my hand along his ass, grabbing and kneading the soft skin. I smirked when he looked back at me with a frustrated, desperate face.

"I've been waiting for this fucking moment for longer than you can imagine, Lennox. Fuck me already."

"Brat," I mumbled before running my cock up and down his crack a few times before settling at his entrance, slowly pushing inside past the muscle trying to keep me out. "Breathe, baby. It's me, okay?" I hoped he emotionally could take it. Physically, I knew he could, even if his face was contouring in pain. He wanted the pain. Needed it.

Cain relaxed more, his head falling forward as I pushed in despite the resistance. I was half inside him when he let out his first groan of pleasure, his fingers gripping the comforter beneath him. "God, you're so fucking tight, Cain. Made for me, just like our Amelia," I told him. I watched as he looked back at me, mouth agape.

"Harder, Lennox. Stop holding back," he demanded. Before he turned around, I pulled my hips back and slammed back into the hilt, grinning. My pelvis slamming into his ass sent him forward, his face burying in the blanket. "That's it. *More*."

I pulled out again and smacked a hand against his ass, hard

enough to leave a fresh pink mark in the shape of my hand. I looked down and admired my handy work. "Stop being so demanding, brat. You'll take what I give you." I pushed back in, deep, sending his body forward again. He reached up and braced himself with both hands on the headboard.

"Fuck yeah, that's it," he moaned. I could tell he was enjoying it by the way he pushed back to meet my punishing thrusts. The sound of skin slapping mixed with the headboard slamming into the wall further encouraged me. I gripped his ass, spreading his cheeks for me and spitting down, adding just a bit of lube. Despite the pain he wanted, I didn't want to seriously hurt him.

"You're doing so good for me, Cain. So warm and fucking tight. You're perfect," I praised. I slapped his ass hard on one cheek, then the other, rotating a few times until his cheeks were bright red and he was screaming. "Touch yourself for me. I want you to come all over this bed before I fill your needy little hole with cum. Do you want that?"

"Yes, yes, yes," he chanted. "Please fill me, Lennox. I want your cum leaking out of my ass when Amelia and Wolf come over."

"Oh, fuck yeah," I groaned. The idea had me pounding into him harder. I was thankful we didn't live with anyone at the rate the headboard crashed into the wall.

Cain left one hand on the headboard while one reached down and started to move up and down his hard cock. He moaned, throwing his head back further. I loved knowing he was working himself, but he set something off in me, and I pushed his hand away to replace it with my own. I gripped tightly, and he jolted, bucking his hips backward into me. I held his hip with my other hand, stilling deep inside him for a moment to jerk him off fast and hard. Cain moaned louder, alternating between cursing and repeating my name until he let loose, shooting cum into my hand, which I further spread along his cock. When he was done and fell into a limp mess on the bed, burying his face in the pillow, I held his hips up and started to fuck him again. He gripped the pillow tightly, his knuckles turning white.

"Fuck, your cock feels so big inside me. I can't wait to feel you fill me up and mark me as yours," Cain muttered into the pillow.

His words set me off, and my orgasm began to tear through me, spreading from my head to my toes as I buried myself inside Cain, spreading his cheeks with my hands as I unloaded inside him. I came harder than I had in my life. I pulled out but kept his cheeks spread, watching as my cum started to drip from his hole and fall onto the comforter. My bed certainly needed a good deep cleaning before I let Amelia on it again.

"Let's get you showered and presentable for Wolf and Amelia. Then I'll invite them over," I told Cain. He shook his head.

"I don't want to shower. I want to make sure I'm dripping while they're here. You and I will know, but they won't."

I smirked, tossing him his clothes so he had something to put on before I called them over. "Dirty, dirty boy."

Amelia

Wolf and I headed to Lennox's place the second he requested us. We were at Wolf's dad's place since his dad worked crazy hours and was hardly home. We had already finished having sex and eating dinner together while we waited. We wanted to give them privacy. We figured they'd cancel on us after they fucked, wanting to spend some time together, so we were surprised when they still called us over.

We discussed any of us messing around without the others days ago and agreed it was fine. Then, Lennox told me his plan to fuck Cain. It wasn't like any of us were officially together, given that I was married to Lennox's dad, but we were all still technically exclusive within the group and agreed upon it. They knew I wasn't doing anything with Henry. Our sham marriage would be over soon; I was sure of it. I made a stupid decision, but now I had people to lose. I needed Lennox, Cain, and Wolf. I didn't need Henry.

I'd tell him I want a divorce. He can keep the fucking inheritance for all I care.

We were surprised to see Lennox and Cain cuddled on the couch when we walked inside Lennox's house. Lennox even had a smile on his face for once, and he was feeding Cain popcorn.

"I see you started without us," I teased, sitting next to Cain, Wolf sitting next to me.

"Oh, we finished without you guys, too," Cain joked, winking at me. I rolled my eyes. I was sure they did, given the smile on Lennox's face.

"So, who topped?" Wolf asked. "We had money on it." I smacked him on the chest.

"I did," Lennox answered. Cain nodded.

"Pay up," I told Wolf, holding out my hand. He groaned and reached into his pocket, grabbing a ten-dollar bill and setting it in my hand. I pocketed it. I called it.

"Can't believe you guys," Cain said, rolling his eyes. "What are we watching tonight?" he asked.

"Guardians Of The Galaxy. The third one just came out, and Wolf hasn't seen any of them," I answered. We decided while they were busy fucking each other's brains out.

I reached over and grabbed the popcorn from Lennox's lap while he found the movie. After he turned it on, he got up from the couch. He returned with snacks and a giant blanket.

"Gummy bears for Wolf, popcorn for all of us, and butterfingers for Amelia," Lennox said, dishing out the snacks. "And I got a giant blanket for us all to share," he said. Lennox was trying the best way he knew how. I never thought I'd forgive him so fast, but I knew he belonged to me. If he could forgive me for stabbing him and marrying his dad, I could forgive him for what happened, too.

We watched the movie silently, all of us eating our snacks before we ended up in strange cuddling positions. Wolf and Cain fell asleep, but I couldn't. I had to be back in time, or Henry would get suspicious. I needed to get myself out of the shithole I dug myself in.

"I need your help, Lennox," I told him as we stood up from the couch, letting the others sleep on it while I prepared to leave. "I need to tell you the entire truth, and we need to discuss everything. Meet me on Thursday at the library, okay? After classes."

"Why can't we talk now?" he asked, cocking a brow.

"There's a lot to discuss between you and me," I responded, turning my head to look at our company. "Some of it they know, some they don't. I'd rather tell you first."

"Fine. I'll meet you Thursday afternoon," he said, stepping toward me. I backed up until I hit the wall, and he boxed me in by placing his hands on either side of my head. He leaned in and pressed his lips against mine in the most gentle kiss he had ever given me. It was a kind of gentle I didn't know he was capable of. Then, he pulled away, leaving me mesmerized by such a simple gesture. "I love you. Now go home to my dad, angel," he said with a grin, winking.

Amelia

I expected Henry to be in bed, not awake, drunk, and playing poker with his friends. He greeted me when I walked in the door, approaching me and speaking quietly to avoid disturbing his friends. "Hello, Wife. Where have you been?" he questioned. His breath smelled like pure liquor, and it disgusted me.

"I—I was out," I struggled to say. I had no excuse made up, so I had to think. "With Lily," I lied. It was entirely reasonable that I'd be hanging out with my only friend. If he knew I was with Lennox and the boys, he might kill me.

He pushed me against the wall, and I winced. I turned away from him, but he leaned closer, sniffing me. "You were with them," he said matter-of-factually. "I told you what would happen if I caught you with them. It's time you're taught a lesson, maybe. If you even so much as tell them anything about our deal or the truth, I won't hesitate to kill them." He ran the back of his finger down my temple and cheek, gripping my chin and making me face him. "Let's go meet some friends."

He walked away, and I followed him into the dining room, where his guests were. They were all wildly drunk and obnoxiously loud. "Guys, this is my wife, Amelia. Amelia, this is Robert, Michael, Jackson, Jacob, and Elliott." He pointed around the table at various men, but I didn't bother to learn their names.

"Robert, Amelia was actually the one who stabbed Lennox," Henry said, laughing and holding a hand on my lower back. I looked at him with wide eyes. He boldly told some guy at his party that I had attempted to kill his son like it was nothing. He was setting me up like he said he would. I was screwed. I hated Henry more than I ever hated Lennox or even my father. He was intelligent and meticulous.

"Well then, you just let me know if you ever get bored and need to press charges," Robert responded, laughing with him. Everyone was slapping their beers together, taking drinks, and having the time of their lives at my expense.

"I'm going to take her to bed quickly, boys. I'll be back." We walked away with his hand on my lower back, and it took all my strength to hold in my snacks and not vomit all over the floor. Henry's small touch made me ill. Agreeing to marry him was the stupidest thing I had ever done. I blame my underdeveloped brain. People my age never made good decisions.

Henry brought me to his room instead of my own. I didn't like the implication. "I want you to head to bed and wait for me. I'll be in eventually. Saturday, I'm going to take you out. A date for you and I. Wear my favorite skirt," he said. He leaned down and kissed me on the top of my head. "Goodnight, Wife. Get to bed." I turned to walk away and get changed, and he smacked my ass. I had only hoped that he wouldn't try to touch me later when he joined me in bed.

I could deal with drunk, needy Henry for one night, but no longer. Once I told Lennox everything, we'd find a way to escape this mess. I couldn't keep my marriage up for the required time. Henry was a delicate situation with his threats lingering over me.

"Have a good night with the boys. I'll see you soon," I responded, giving him a fake smile. He left the room, leaving me alone to change. I had nothing to wear, so I snuck into my room to throw on pajama pants and a shirt. I climbed into bed as requested, and thankfully, I was passed out by the time he joined me. Surprisingly, touching a sleeping girl seemed against Henry's beliefs.

Amelia

Before I reached the library, a douchebag I had never spoken to backed me into a wall, his upper body pressing against mine. I turned my cheek to him, not wanting to be face-to-face. My back hurt from the blow it took being forced against the cold stone wall.

"The campus whore, all alone in the hallway. Must be my lucky day." His fingers ran along my arm, trailing to grip my hip. "I heard you're a come dumpster. Do you want my come, you filthy whore?" He placed an arm around me, pulling my lower half against his and revealing his disgusting hard-on while grinding it on me.

"What I really want is you to brush your teeth," I grit out, refusing to turn my head.

The way he caught me angered me because I couldn't reach my knife. I had to hope someone came along soon and stopped this. My body froze, reminding me of the times in the halls at my high school. It was a similar experience there. I felt helpless all over again. Even if I could stab him, I wasn't sure my body could react. I was shutting down. Lennox had truly ruined me.

The man gripped my throat tightly, taking my breath away in the worst way. I choked in his grasp while his face turned red. "You're going to pay for that comment, bitch," he promised, a grin taking over his face.

"Logan Hunt, get your fucking hands off my stepmom," Lennox's voice said.

Of course, he knew where I was going. The guys never left me alone for more than an hour. Normally, his appearance would be annoying. Right now, it was more than welcome.

"Your...what?" Logan said, wide-eyed. He released my throat, and I bent over, gasping for air and coughing. Lennox ran to my side.

"She married my dad, the dean, you dense fuck."

"But—you—you said to hurt her. So, I did," Logan pleaded. He was terrified of what Lennox would do. Logan fucked up. My marriage was common knowledge, and somehow he missed out. I didn't feel bad for him. He was willing to sexually assault me in a school hallway.

"No one fucking touches her," Lennox said. "I'm going to use you to send the message." He stalked toward a frozen Logan. I walked away but stayed nearby to watch Lennox pummel Logan's ass into the floor. Lennox knocked him to the ground with one hit, then sat on top of him and held him by the shirt, punching his face bloody. Blood splattered onto Lennox, the floor, and the walls. Something about him beating the shit out of a man in my honor turned me on.

"Lennox!" I heard Henry's voice bellow from several feet away. Lennox stopped wailing into the kid and jumped off him, his breathing ragged. Logan groaned from the floor, his face unrecognizable.

"He's lucky I didn't kill him," Lennox muttered.

His fists were already ruined before; now, they were beyond fucked up. He needed to put a stop to his fighting for a while. Not that he'd listen to me.

"He tried to attack Amelia," Lennox said. He didn't know that Henry hated me and wanted nothing more than to torment me for revenge. Someone in that family constantly wanted revenge on me.

"Oh. Well, good job then," Henry commended. "I'll call security and get them to come take care of him. Get out of here." He waved Lennox off, and Lennox gave me a sympathetic look before running off at his father's command.

"What were you doing here with Lennox?" Henry asked, taking a few steps closer toward me. "I warned you. Don't have a relationship with him or his friends. You're mine now until I say otherwise." He backed me into the wall but kept his hands off me.

"I was headed to study, and Lennox came out of nowhere. I— I'm sorry." I didn't recognize my weak voice as my own. Since when did I apologize to men when I did nothing wrong? Why was I afraid of Henry? I feared him more than I ever feared his son.

"Go home and make me dinner, wife," Henry directed, backing away and waving me off.

I nodded and listened.

Lennox

I took advantage of my dad being at dinner by checking Amelia's location. She wasn't with him; she was at home. Despite staying back at my mom's house, I took any chance I could to try to see her. We hadn't had sex since the night we shared her, and I wanted her again, badly. I wasn't sure she wanted me, but I had to try.

When I approached the house, I didn't give a shit about cameras finding me. I had every reason to be at my father's house. I could easily pretend I forgot he was gone. I still had a key to get inside. I hoped she wasn't in her room so I could avoid the hallway cameras. Thanks to Wolf, we knew the blind spots in the house. Because my dad was obsessed with keeping people out of her room, most of the house was a blind spot.

When I walked in, Amelia was in the kitchen. She looked at me wide-eyed and dropped the spoon in her hand. My dad was out to eat at an expensive steakhouse, and she was eating a bowl of cereal.

"Lennox?" she questioned in a disbelieving voice.

"I got your text message, Angel. What do you need from me that the others can't give you?" I asked, stalking toward her.

She tried to walk away. I pushed her back toward the counter with my body, then gripped the counter and boxed her in. She refused to look me in the eye, opting to look at the floor instead. I smirked, happy I had her flustered. Whatever she wanted to say, she was apprehensive to say it.

"We can talk about this later," she said, looking toward the ground. "I don't want to get in trouble when your father walks in," she whispered. Whatever he conditioned her to believe, she was terrified something would happen to her if we got caught. Their marriage was a sham—so why would he care?

"We can talk about this now. He's not coming home anytime soon. He's out with friends, probably getting drunk on expensive champagne right now," I reassured her. I knew how my dad's dinners went. "The Amelia I know is a force to be reckoned with, not a shy girl who refuses to go for what she wants." She looked up at me with a sharp warning glance. I smiled, knowing I had her attention.

"After all we've been through…it's an odd request. I'm nervous, okay?" she gritted, clenching her jaw. "What if it sets us backward? What if I can't handle what you say?" she said quietly.

The corner of my mouth raised when I realized what she was saying. There was only one thing she'd be ashamed to ask for, one thing the others couldn't give her as good as I could. I placed my hand on her thigh, watching as her breath hitched in response. I snaked it to the back of her thigh, sliding my hand up and grabbing a handful of her ass. "My dirty girl wants to be told how much of a whore she is for me?" I asked, my eyes intently watching her body's reaction.

She moaned softly, her lips parting. I swiped my hand along her slit to feel the wetness gathered. "Fuck," I mumbled. I pushed her panties aside to run my finger along her slit. She faltered in my arms, but I held her up by pressing my body

against hers. "That's my good little whore, getting wet for me."
She groaned.

"You told me girls would run from sex with you. I didn't see
that side of you...but I want to," she pleaded quietly.

"You're sure you're ready for that?" I whispered near her ear,
teasing her by slipping a finger into her pussy before pulling it
out and sucking the finger clean.

She nodded her head. "I remember my safe word for if it's
too much."

I gripped her throat tight and squeezed at the sides. Her eyes
widened in surprise, her mouth opening as she blinked a few
times. I smirked and tilted my head. "You'll take it, Angel. I
know you can."

"Don't hold back," she instructed. I didn't plan to.

I let go of her throat and grabbed her hand, walking her
toward the dining room table. I wanted to take her to a place
she often ate dinner with my piece of shit father. I wanted her
to remember this table for good reasons beyond when he made
her cook for him. I hated how he treated Amelia. She deserved
the world, but we all treated her like shit. My father was the
man who she trusted to help her. She had to learn the hard
way he wasn't a man of his word; he was a man of bending his
promises.

I kissed her while backing her ass into the table, then I pulled
away and spun her around so her hips were against the edge
of the table. I pushed her forward, pressing her face into the
wooden surface. Her whimpering went straight to my cock. I
loved to listen to her struggle. No matter how much I loved her,
my kinks would never change. I could tell she liked it because
she ground her ass against my cock.

"Such a slut, prancing around the house in this tiny skirt,

begging to be fucked," I told her gruffly. I undid my belt and let my pants drop to the ground while pushing her skirt up to her hips. "My naughty little angel." I ran my finger along her slit, pleased to feel her wetness gathering. "You're so wet already." My cock hardened at the finding.

I pulled my boxers down and kneeled, inhaling her scent before spreading her cheeks and burying my tongue in her pussy. I savored the taste of her on my tongue. I couldn't believe I spent so long missing out on this. She tasted like Heaven and sin.

She moaned into the table, and I pulled away, stroking my cock a few times while staring at her. She was picturesque from behind. I wanted to take her beautiful ass, but I missed her pussy and needed to be buried inside her. It wasn't like we had a lot of time.

I ran the tip of my dick along her slick slit, gathering juices before slamming myself inside in one hard thrust. The table moved with the force of my thrusting, her hips slamming into the wooden table hard enough to bruise. I gripped the back of her neck harshly, keeping her cheek against the table as I pistoned into her at a brutal pace. I needed to leave my marks on her body and remind her who she belonged to. Her moans turned silent as I held her throat, and then I let go after a few seconds to allow her to breathe. I listened to her struggle for air. She bucked her hips backward, making sure I was balls deep with each thrust. I spread her cheeks, spitting on her asshole.

"Does my dirty whore want her ass filled, too?"

Her nails scratched the table as she moaned louder, the sound of my hips slamming into her ass loudly filling the room. "Yes!" she screamed.

I slipped a finger inside her back hole, teasing the entrance.

"Tell me you're a slut, and I'll give you what you want," I promised.

"I'm a slut," she moaned. I shifted my angle to hit her G-spot as a reward. "Oh, fuck. I'm a fucking slut for you."

I groaned. I pushed my finger in her ass to my knuckle, pumping in and out a few times before adding a second one. She was a moaning, writhing mess, her ass shifting up to allow me to hit her deeper inside. I took my other hand and placed a few hard smacks on her ass cheek until her beautiful ivory skin turned a pretty red color.

I aggressively fingered her backside in tandem with my punishing thrusts until I pulled my fingers out. I used that hand to grasp her hips and fuck her harder into the table, my other hand snaking up and pushing three fingers into her mouth, gripping her jaw roughly from the inside. She gagged and coughed around my fingers, her spit falling from the corners of her mouth. I withdrew my fingers and let her breathe.

"You look so fucking beautiful falling apart on my cock, Angel."

"More. Harder," she pleaded.

I let go of her hip and fisted her hair, pulling her back so her back was pressed against my chest. "Dirty fucking whore. You're insatiable. Is that why you need three cocks?" I stopped my thrusts and listened to her moans of frustration. I grinned. Moving my hand between us, I slotted my fingers at her entrance, slowly easing them inside with my cock. Her pussy gripped me like a vice. I knew she'd like the extra full sensation.

"Oh, fuck. Oh God," she moaned, leaning her head back against my shoulder as she pushed back, sending me further inside her.

"God isn't here, baby; I'm the devil. Fuck yourself on my hand and cock," I directed.

Amelia pushed her hips back until she was filled to the hilt. Her body wriggled in an attempt to get away, but she moaned loudly, her beautiful sounds filling the air.

"That's right. Take what you need. My beautiful, greedy slut," I whispered in her ear.

I felt her pussy tightening and knew she was on the verge of an orgasm. It was rare that she'd orgasm without clitoral stimulation, but I was glad to be the one to bring her to that point. I wrapped my free hand around the front of her throat, squeezing the sides. Her moans turned into screams as she squeezed the life out of my cock, tightening around me as her orgasm slammed into her. I gripped her throat tighter as I felt her come on my cock and fingers, the sensation driving me wild. I released her throat and pushed her against the table again, holding her face there with the fingers that were inside her pussy seconds ago. I pounded into her at a punishing pace before stilling while buried deep, filling her with my come as I moaned. Weeks without sex was the longest I went, but it was worth it to wait for her. I didn't want anyone else touching me. My cock kept pumping come, and when I pulled out, I watched it drip from between her legs.

"Remember that if my father fucks you tonight. He's going to feel my come inside of you, filthy girl." I watched as she breathed heavily against the table. I held her hips to ensure she didn't fall, my own breathing a struggle.

"He'll never touch me, Lennox. Only you, Cain, and Wolf are allowed to touch me. I promise no one else will."

"Oh, I know. If anyone else ever touches you, we'll kill them, Angel. You're ours, forever, no matter what the law says. Now,

I have somewhere I need to take you. Let's go."

Amelia

When I got into Lennox's car, I was skeptical. I had no idea where he was taking me. We drove to the other side of town, a place we never went to together before, and I was sure he was planning to murder me and dispose of my body. My suspicions arose further when we exited the car at a lake outside town. It wasn't some beautiful, picturesque lake from a movie scene. It was a dull, man-made, small lake set near train tracks. The train tracks were a part of a former train station, and the area had been riddled with graffiti since closing.

We walked along the short dock and sat at the edge. I had no idea Lennox's plans, and he still didn't talk to me. Distantly, the sun was setting behind us. It was still a pretty sight, even if the lake looked like a dumping ground for toxic waste.

"Is this where you finally kill me to take your revenge?" I joked, but his silence frightened me until his lips curled into a small smile.

"If I planned to kill you already, you'd be dead," he said, laughing.

"I think it's the same for me. I wouldn't have missed any vital organs or arteries unless my heart truly wanted me to miss," I said, hitting his shoulder with mine. "Even if I hated you, I loved you. I couldn't imagine my life without you, even if it meant dealing with your torment for the rest of my life." Sadly, I meant it. He could've tormented me further, but he didn't. Not until the end did I set him off.

"What did you mean about my mom?" he asked softly, looking down at his feet hanging just above the water.

"Lennox...I can't say anything right now, okay?" I sighed. I felt bad. He deserved to know the truth about his family. I'm sure, in some way, he already did. But someone needed to tell him outright. I couldn't risk their lives by saying anything. I had to play by Henry's rules.

"She's my mom, Amelia. You're saying she did something bad. I deserve to know." He laid his head on my shoulder, his feet still dangling over the lake. I would've dipped my feet in if I felt the water was safe. I hated big bodies of water overall and had a distrust of them.

"I know. I know. I promise I'll explain everything soon. I'm married to Henry out of convenience, but I promise I want out of it. I promise I love you, Cain, and Wolf. Not Henry. I swear I'm protecting all of us," I explained, running my fingers through his hair. "Just know...I don't agree with how my Dad handled things."

He sighed. He sat up, reached into his pocket, and handed me a knife in a bag. The knife had blood on it, and I quickly recognized it as mine. My eyes widened. "Here's the knife we used to blackmail you. I promise it's the only evidence we have. You...you never killed that man. Cain did. Then, he found what you used to stab him, and we framed you to blackmail you. We wanted you, and I wanted revenge at the same time. I'm so sorry. I'm an idiot. Please forgive me, angel."

"Relax," I told him when his voice started to get frantic. "I fucked with you guys, too. We let something from years ago ruin us. Something our parents did. It means a lot to me that you're giving me an out, babe, but I'm still here. Blackmail or not, I'm yours."

'Good. I can't imagine a life without you, Amelia. I'd kill myself if you asked me to; that's how much I need you."

"If you told me that weeks ago, I could've gotten my revenge," I teased. I looked at the weapon several times before chucking it into the lake. I was sure the lake held many secrets. "A fresh start for us."

Cain

It was two in the morning when we showed up at Amelia's window. I turned to Lennox before we climbed up her wooden ladder. "You took care of the issue, right?" I asked in reference to Henry. I hoped Henry wasn't suspicious enough to avoid drinking anything from Lennox since it was odd for his son to ask him out to dinner. Other than that, I trusted that Lennox would've told us if his mission failed. But part of me wondered if he wanted his dad to catch him with Amelia.

Lennox held up a bottle of sleeping pills and shook it. "It's done. She's ours. Not that I give a shit if he hears."

I was the first to start climbing since I had the most experience sneaking into her room at night. I loved watching her, and it was a bit easier here. We had a ladder directly to her room. It was like Henry wanted us to slip up.

I opened the window and stepped onto the floor with no issues. Wolf came behind me, struggling and falling to the floor with a thud. I laughed. It was easy, but he made it seem hard.

"I don't know how you do this all the time," Wolf said, shaking his head and dusting himself off when he stood.

"It's easy, dipshit," Lennox said, stepping into the room with ease. Wolf rolled his eyes. "Now, did our princess wake up?" he asked.

We looked over toward her. She was still asleep, which we wanted. We had plans to wake her up in the best way possible. She was a heavy sleeper but a loud screamer, so we had to drug Henry. Something about sneaking into his house and fucking his wife while he was out was hot.

I even brought a knife to play. I had a plan.

I laid on the bed between her legs, pulling down her pajama pants and underwear to expose her to us. I inhaled her scent before licking up her cunt, my tongue pressing circles around her clit before sucking it into my mouth. Amelia took her sleeping medication tonight, I could tell, but she still groaned for me, her wetness beginning to hit my chin.

I loved burying my face in Amelia's warm, wet pussy. I loved the whimpers she made and the way her body recognized me even when she was asleep.

Lennox stood at the edge of the bed, lifting her shirt and lightly teasing her nipples. She'd be awake soon. No one could sleep through the sensations we had to be giving her. I thought about everything I wanted to do to her and thrust a finger inside her, preparing her for us. We'd all have her at the same time. We planned this. We needed her.

I curled my fingers upward to hit the spot she loved, and her hips bucked, her eyes opening with a loud moan. "Oh, God," she breathed. She looked down at me with groggy eyes, her fingers gripping the sheets tight. "Fuck, Cain," she mumbled.

I inserted another finger, then added one into her back hole, opening her up on both ends for us. She writhed and moaned, tossing in the sheets. She bit her lip, trying to keep quiet. "Henry..." she said. Hearing his name with my fingers inside her made me physically ill. Letting the anger fuel me, I pushed my fingers inside her harder, her hips fighting to move off the bed.

"Passed out, angel," Lennox told her. "He won't be waking up anytime soon," he promised.

"Who do you want in your ass, baby? We decided to let you choose where we all go," I told her. She made soft, sleepy, mumbling sounds between breathy moans. I bit her thigh to get her attention, hoping she'd come out of her trance. I didn't care if she fell asleep soon, but I needed her awake enough to answer my question.

"Wolf," she muttered. "Cain in my pussy and Lennox in my mouth." The words sounded like a plea from her lustful tone. Hearing my name from her mouth caused my cock to harden against my zipper. I sucked her clit a few more times, hard, before pulling away.

I heard a commotion next to me but paid no attention while I continued to curl my fingers and move them against Amelia's G-spot. I wanted to watch her face while she came, and I could tell she was close. She had telltale signs like the way she clenched her walls as if to keep me in, the whimpers that escaped her mouth faster, and how she threw her head back. "Look at me, Little Thorn," I demanded.

Wolf lay next to her on the bed, suddenly naked and face-up. I heard a slurping sound and noticed Lennox between Wolf's legs out of the corner of my eye, but I didn't break eye contact with Amelia.

"Come for me, my love," I told her. I watched with a smirk as she fell apart around me, her pussy suffocating my fingers, her eyes closing. Her hips moved, sending my fingers further inside as she rode out her orgasm with loud moans.

"Oh, God, Cain. Right fucking there." I bit down on her clit until she started to pull away from me, pushing my head away with her hand. I smirked against her pussy before pulling back my fingers, letting her catch her breath on the bed.

Lennox poured lube into his hand and started to work Wolf's cock to prepare him for Amelia. I took the lube from the bed and spread it on my fingers.

"Come here, Amelia," I said. "Ass toward me."

She obliged, and I slowly worked two fingers into her tight, puckered hole to work the lube around. Her fingers squeezed the sheets underneath her until her knuckles were white. "Does it feel okay?" I asked.

"Yes," she responded breathlessly. "I need more."

"I think you're ready for us, angel," Lennox said. He stood up from the bed and stripped his clothing before moving to me, sensually pulling up my shirt and running his hand down my chest and abs, unbuttoning my pants and pulling them down. "Get on top of Wolf and ride him, baby. Facing up."

Amelia hovered above Wolf with her back facing him before reaching between them and grabbing his cock, then settling it at her back entrance. She sank down and slowly pushed down, and I watched as her ass swallowed his length inch by inch. Wolf and Amelia both moaned when her ass connected with his pelvis.

"Lay back," I told her, ready to join the fun. She did as told and laid her back to Wolf's chest. My eyes stayed at the spot where they connected, watching him slowly start moving in and out of her. It was a beautiful sight, one that I'd be a part of in a moment. I knew it'd feel good to feel Wolf rubbing my cock through the thin barrier. I almost wished we were sharing the same hole. It would feel so fucking good to have him rub against me in her tight little hole. We'd explore that another time, though.

Lennox crawled onto the bed, placing his knees on either side of Amelia's head, his ass toward me. "Ready for my cock, angel?" Lennox asked her. She didn't have time to respond. When she opened her mouth to answer, he slid past her lips, leaning forward and bracing himself by placing his palms on the bed. "Beautiful," he mumbled, letting out a moan. I knew what it felt like to have that sweet mouth wrapped around your cock.

Wolf and Lennox were in a slow rhythm, but they halted to wait for me to join. I lined myself up with her entrance, rubbing the head of my cock against her juices first, then pushed inside to the hilt. Burying myself inside of her was still the sweetest feeling. She felt like home, and now they all did.

"You're doing so good taking all of us, Little Thorn," I cooed, not that she could respond with the way I could see Lennox buried so far in her throat. "I wish you could see how beautiful you look."

"God, she's so fucking tight," Wolf moaned. We thrust in tandem, our cocks hitting each other through the thin barrier. "And you feel so fucking good against my cock," he told me. Fuck. I loved being closer to Wolf now, but I wished there was no barrier. All of us being together felt right.

"Her mouth is still perfect," Lennox said, thrusting into her while she lay on top of Wolf. I had the beautiful sight of Lennox's ass and how it flexed with each push of his hips.

I had a crazy idea and put my plan in motion by leaning forward, my tongue running along Lennox's tight hole, rimming him. I groaned into his crack, slowly pushing my tongue inside. Lennox stopped his thrusting and held his position.

"Oh, *fuck*. That feels so fucking good, Cain. I'm not going to last." The normally tough Lennox sounded whiny and needy, which was music to my ears.

"Harder," Amelia mumbled around Lennox's length.

I smirked." You heard her, boys."

Lennox started to move his hips again, thrusting into her harder until she began to gag around him, while Wolf and I kept our slow pace but slammed into her hard, the bed rocking into the wall each time. I loved the sound of the wood smacking the drywall, which reminded me of how carnal we were together.

I pulled my mouth away from Lennox's puckered hole and replaced it with a finger. His back bowed, his head falling back. "Jesus fucking Christ. Oh, God. Right there," he moaned while I repeatedly hit his prostate. I leaned down and bit his ass cheek, and he stilled inside Amelia's mouth and came with a howl.

"Mmm, I love making you fall apart, baby," I told him. He popped out of Amelia's mouth, his ass moving backward and chasing my fingers as he rode through his orgasm, clenching around me. His cum flowed down Amelia's mouth, mixing with her drool and tears, and I had never seen anything more stunning. My hips started to piston faster, and I threw my head back as I enjoyed the sensation of Amelia's tight pussy, and rubbing against Wolf.

"God, you guys make me feel so fucking good," Amelia said.

"Lennox, hand it to me," I said. He knew what I meant, but Amelia cocked a brow.

He handed me my knife, and I flicked it open and placed it in Amelia's hand. 'I want you to carve your initials in me, Little Thorn. Please," I begged. I had this plan—a way to help atone for my sins against her. I couldn't forget how I hurt her before I knew the lengths I'd go to to protect her, even from Lennox. No matter what she did to me, I loved her—needed her. Craved her.

Amelia wasted no time carving her initials into my chest. The knife made the three lines for the A, and I grunted, my face tight as I tried to forget about the pain. It helped to see my blood drip onto her chest. I reached down and spread it into the skin on her chest, pinching her nipples in the process. "I love you," she said in a moan. "I love marking your skin, marking you as my property."

"I'm all yours," I mumbled, my thrusts becoming erratic and crazed. As much as the knife hurt, I took pleasure in the feeling, and it brought me to orgasm as I spilled my cum inside her. "I can't wait to fill you with our baby one day. I'm going to pump you full of my cum when your birth control expires."

She must've liked my words because she clenched my cock hard, spiraling into her second orgasm of the night. I stopped my thrusts as I continued to pump her full of my cum, then I pulled out of her and watched it drop out of her and onto where she connected with Wolf.

"I'm close. My turn," Wolf said. "Flip around so you can mark me."

Amelia sat up and turned around to face him, sitting with his cock buried in her ass as she rested her palms on his chest. The bloody knife rested on the bed. She picked it up again and started to carve her initials into Wolf's chest. Before she had the A finished, he stilled, spilling his seed in her tight ass as he moaned and cursed loudly.

"It hurts...so good..." he said.

Once she was done with her initials, she leaned down and licked some of the blood before pulling herself off and collapsing on the bed next to him. "Fuck, that felt so good."

"Where's my mark, angel?" Lennox asked, climbing on the bed next to her. "I want a reminder of you every time I look

97

into the mirror."

She smirked, turning on her side to face him. "I thought you wouldn't want your pretty little skin all bloody," she told him.

"Bring it on, mama," he said, winking. I loved watching their newfound banter. Things were better now between all of us. I watched as she repeated with Lennox what she had already done to us. While she carved the skin on his chest, I took out bandages from the bag we brought, placing one on me and one on Wolf. I brought one to Lennox when she was complete.

"Let's get you in the shower, and Lennox will clean up these sheets," I told Amelia. I reached down and pushed the hair from her face, smiling down at her. Wolf walked to the connected bathroom and turned on the water. I picked her up when the water stopped and placed her into the tub. I bathed and changed her until we had to leave, afraid Henry would wake up soon.

Amelia

I hated the idea of being in public with Henry, but I needed to behave for him. It made me laugh thinking about how Lennox could never make me obey him like he wanted, but Henry easily could. Henry stirred fear in me, unlike his son. His son was better at stirring arousal. Here I was, Saturday night, compliant with Henry's wishes. I'm in a skirt with my hair curled, bright red lipstick, and a top he picked out for me. I had fifteen minutes before he'd be here to pick me up with his driver.

After Lennox handed me the weapon back—which was thankfully in the lake by now—I knew things needed to change for the better. He finally gave me all of him. He groveled enough. He proved himself to me, and it meant the world to me.

It was rare that Henry took me out. He demanded I cook for him most days. He had a list of meals he preferred, too. He had enough money to hire someone else to cook his meals, but it was a power play. Henry wanted to own me and show me that he owned me. He wanted the picture-perfect life in the eyes of his peers: an attractive, young wife who took care of him. If only they knew he spent his "honeymoon" with other women in Europe.

Scratch that. Men like him? They wouldn't care. They probably wouldn't be surprised to hear he bought me as a child.

I saw Henry's black Aston Martin pull into the circular driveway, and it was my queue to head out. I walked down the stairs and let myself out the front door, joining Henry in the backseat of the car.

"Your outfit is fine," he said, taking a quick look at me before burying himself in paperwork again. He was the one who told me what to wear but didn't seem enthusiastic about what he chose. Even on the way to dinner, he couldn't give up work. It wasn't like it was a romantic outing, though. And it wasn't like anyone was watching us here, so there was no need to keep up the image. The driver and I made eye contact through the rearview mirror, though.

"Thank you," I said, unsure of anything else to say. I hated being alone with him, especially in a small car. He had his work to focus on while I stared out the window.

He took me to a nice restaurant on the edge of town, but we never went inside. We stopped in an alley behind the place and exited the car. He nodded to his driver, and he drove off, leaving us standing outside alone.

"Why are we back here, Henry?" I asked.

I backed away slowly, looking around for an exit. The situation was odd, and I didn't trust Henry. My breathing picked up, sweat pooling in my palms. I felt the adrenaline spike telling me I was in danger—a cruel smirk formed on Henry's lips.

"I told you you'd be punished, Amelia. You'll learn to appreciate me, but it'll be too late. I told Levi he can do whatever he wants with you. I told him to break you. Did you think I only put cameras where you'd see them?" His lips curled further, a fit of laughter taking over. "I'm not stupid. I know you fucked them despite my warning. You'll pay for that now."

I heard tires screeching behind me, then the sound of doors slamming. I felt strong arms grab me on each side and the sharp prick of a needle in my arm before things went dark.

Amelia

"You know...Henry said I could break you in however I wish. You're going to auction in a month. You need to be trained first," Levi said. His eyes darkened as he looked at me, licking his lips. "It's a bonus that you've got my boys distracted. They think they're too good for me now. They want to go back to their trust funds. I'll take away the only thing they cared about, and they'll step back in line," he explained. His reasoning was stupid. He'd only be angering them enough to murder him, but I wasn't going to explain that. He could deal with the consequences himself.

"You can't break me, Levi. I spent years being forced to give blowjobs to the perviest, most disgusting older men at my boarding school. It only turned me into a needy whore who couldn't keep her legs shut, as Henry pointed out," I said with a smirk.

"It's going to be a lot worse than taking some cocks in your mouth, Little Girl. I'm going to have men come in here and fuck your drugged pussy, ass, or mouth every day. It starts with me." Levi was the main supplier of the drug I had been given at my first party in town. Cain said the sexual effects would only work if you were attracted to someone. I hoped he was wrong because if I was going to put up with being raped until someone found me, I wanted to forget or enjoy it. "Such a pretty skirt," he cooed, eyeing me up and down from my position on the bed. My hands were above my head, hooked onto a heavy-duty chain I could hardly move. I felt uncomfortable at his stare, but I had nowhere to go. I regretted wearing the skirt. Henry bought it and told me he was taking me out for a nice dinner. I should've known something was up. Henry wasn't generous. He made it clear he wanted me around so he could destroy me.

Levi pushed the dress to my hips, exposing my pink lace underwear. Warmth flooded my cheeks. The bed dipped as he joined me, pulling down my underwear and exposing me to the cool air. "I'll admit, you have a pretty pussy, but it can't be that great." He huffed. "I inspect all my girls. Sometimes, I have a little taste."

He leaned down and inhaled my scent before dipping a finger inside. I wished he had given me drugs already so I didn't have to be awake and remember this moment. I felt disgusting as my pussy clenched around his fingers, aware there was a strange intruder inside. My body rejected his touch. He brought the finger to his mouth, sucking it clean. "Damn, Raven. I can see why they're all distracted."

"Raven?" I questioned, cocking my head.

"The name suits you. You'll need a new one for when we auction you at the club. Amelia Perkins won't exist anymore, but Raven will." His explanation made me gag. I'd never see the auction. Cain, Lennox, and Wolf would save me before anything happened.

With my underwear pulled off and my dress hitched, my legs were free. He stupidly didn't have them attached to the bed. I used my freedom to kick him as hard as I could, wherever I could land a hit and ended up getting him in the stomach. He jumped off the bed and keeled over.

"Axel!" Levi screamed, groaning as he clutched his stomach. I smiled, proud of myself. I hoped I fought him off enough to remain untouched by him, but I knew he'd be angry enough to potentially make someone else take over. I wasn't thinking when I kicked him since I couldn't go anywhere after. Not unless I mustered up the strength to rip off industrial strength hooks.

The guard from earlier who had helped chain me walked in. He looked between the two of us. His urge was to go to Levi first, but Levi held a hand in the air. "Just punish her," he instructed. Axel—also known as Bigfoot, given his size— stalked to my side, a bitter frown on his face. It wasn't like he looked happy before, but I had never seen such a large man expressionless yet angry.

"Got it, boss," he said.

"And chain her damn legs." Levi sighed.

I kicked the air wildly, but it didn't help. Axel caught my legs and cuffed them, attaching them to the chains at the base of the bed. Then, he looked at me with a menacing grin. "I'm going to enjoy this," he told me.

I knew I wasn't.

Axel walked to a standing wardrobe at the other end of the room and grabbed something from it that I couldn't see. When he came into view, he held a whip in his hand. I wriggled in the chains, but it was helpless. It wasn't like I'd be able to get out of them. Axel wore a dark grin that terrified me.

"Ready for your punishment?" he asked.

Before I could answer, he whipped my leg, and I whimpered. Pain shot through my body at the harsh contact.

"Stop! They'll fucking kill you, I promise you," I shouted.

Anything to get him to stop. My words didn't work. He actually fucking grinned like he'd enjoy it more.

"I wish I could smack your ass so bad," he said, whipping my stomach a few times. I winced but tried my best not to react anymore. If I did, he'd enjoy it. I didn't want him to win. Truthfully, I wasn't sure if lashing me or raping me would've been worse. I took the rest of my lashes silently, not wanting to anger or please him. He stopped after another five, realizing I wasn't reacting.

"Mark her," Levi directed. "Number eighty-two."

Axel grinned, walked to the counter, grabbed a tattoo gun, and came back. I tried to move, but it wasn't much help.

"Don't do that, or it'll be fucked up," he advised.

I heard the buzzing of the tattoo gun seconds before I felt the pain from the needle, but the tattoo only lasted a few seconds.

"I was going to give you a free day to adjust. Thanks to your behavior, I'm going to send someone in tomorrow. My men are going to love breaking you in," Levi said. He lifted himself from his spot on the floor and left the room. Axel followed shortly behind him, and I sighed in relief when they left the room, and I heard the door lock.

Lennox

I went to my dad's house to catch a glimpse of Amelia, but I came up with a lie to tell him so he wouldn't get suspicious. It wasn't like he didn't know what we had done before, but he couldn't know anything was happening now.

I knew he took her out to dinner. He said he was taking her out for a nice date at a special place. Amelia got hives just talking about it earlier. She didn't trust him, rightfully so. I wondered why he'd want to take her out in the first place. They often ate at home. My dad could afford a chef, but he was too traditional. He wanted a wife to do the housework for him. It was only a matter of time before he made Amelia quit school and become a full-time wife. I hoped she got out of the marriage before that.

The front door slammed, and my dad entered the kitchen, stopping in his tracks when he saw me. A smile formed on his lips. "Lennox, son. What did I do to deserve the pleasure of your company?" he asked. He set down his briefcase and phone on the counter and walked to the refrigerator, getting a glass of water and chugging it down.

"Where's Amelia?" I asked.

"Why are you asking about my wife?" Henry questioned in a taunting tone, cocking his head.

I wasn't initially suspicious that he had done anything to her, but his response made me wonder. I studied his face, but he kept it the same, not giving anything away. I walked closer to him, standing at his side. "Just wondering where she went after dinner is all," I responded.

"Girls night. I dropped her off with her little friend...Lily or whatever," he answered, except his eyes looked away when he responded.

My father was a decent-sized man, but he went down quickly with one punch to the face. I'd do anything for Amelia, including channeling strength I didn't have.

I immediately dialed Cain and had him come over, and he was there within minutes, helping me drag my father downstairs and strap him to a chair.

"What's next?" Cain asked.

"You leave. I'll ask him questions when he wakes up," I answered. I had to think about what to ask and how to respond. One wrong move and Amelia's whereabouts were in the dust.

"Are you sure? You don't have to do this alone, brother."

"I'm sure." I nodded. "Go tell Wolf that she's missing. Start trying to track down her location." The best thing Cain could do was relay the message to Wolf. Time mattered in missing persons cases. We knew my father had done something with her. He could've sold her on the black market or buried her alive somewhere by now.

Cain nodded and rushed out of the room. I waited around for my father to come to, and it took roughly an hour before he groaned awake. His head slowly lifted, and he made eye contact with me, another smile forming. "I've never been more proud to call you my son," he said, laughing until he choked and spit out blood.

"Where is Amelia?" I asked, gripping the knife in my hand tighter.

"Watch out, son. Stab me too hard, and you'll never see her again. Though, I doubt you will," he said, chuckling. "I'll punish my wife how I see fit. It doesn't concern you."

"She's your wife for whatever reason, but she's in love with me," I responded.

"But I'm the one who took her virginity when she was twelve." The smile on his face turned upward, an ear-to-ear grin spreading. He was proud of raping a child. My best friend. The love of my life. "And God did her tight, virgin pussy feel good."

I wanted to make him hurt. Logic wasn't controlling me when I reached out and stabbed my knife into his thigh. My subconscious made sure to avoid a major artery, though. I left my knife in there to make sure he didn't bleed out, though.

"You fucking asshole!" My dad yelled between his screams of pain.

"She was a *child*!" Anger filled me. Anger for her, for me, and for the life we lost because of his actions. Anger for my mother, too. "You were married to mom."

"Why do you think I married her, controlled her, and sold her to Levi? To avenge your mother. She went through hell because of her father and how that little bitch seduced me. Her father raped your mom because of what happened. You know your mom didn't deserve it."

"You're a sick, twisted fuck," I said, spitting on his face. "I can't believe I'm your son."

"Where do you think you get it from?" he asked.

"Where. Is. She?" I asked, speaking slowly and angrily.

"I don't know. Levi took her, but he didn't give me details.

All I know is he's involved in sex trafficking. It's where the money is, I'm told." Even after being stabbed, he had the same smug smile.

I pulled the knife, his screams making me happy. I was prepared to stab him again, but my phone had an emergency meeting text. I ripped the sleeves off my shirt and covered his stab wound before leaving the basement and my home, leaving to meet with Wolf and Cain.

Cain

Amelia is gone. He doesn't know where she is.

I read Lennox's text repeatedly, wondering what I could've done differently. She had been gone for a few days, and we had no clue where she was. She went out to dinner with Henry, but only he returned. He didn't tell us shit, so we kept him locked up in the basement. He caved pretty quickly, but his information came with nothing. He said Levi had her but didn't say where he took her. Levi left town with her. We had no tracking devices on either of them, for whatever fucking reason.

I followed her most days but didn't want to see her out to eat with Henry. Why didn't I fucking follow her? I could've stopped all of this. Wolf locked himself up in his room, trying everything he could to find her. He hacked into security cameras and still saw no sign of her beyond getting into a car with three men who took her kicking and screaming. Henry stood by and watched.

I heard a pounding on my door and pulled up my security camera. Lennox and Wolf were at my door. I groaned. They had each tried to call me, but I didn't pick up. I wanted to wallow alone. It was my fault that Henry retaliated and that Levi went along with Henry's plan. He was mad at us for trying

110

to leave him.

I walked downstairs and opened the door, letting them in and locking it behind them. "What the fuck do you guys want?" I asked, sitting on the couch.

"There's something you guys need to know," Wolf said, pacing around the room. "I should've told you sooner but couldn't break her trust." Wolf's pacing was driving me insane. I needed him to get to the point if it involved our Amelia.

"What is it, Wolf?" I asked. "Stop pacing and sit down." He took a seat next to me, breathing deeply.

"Henry raped Amelia when she was twelve. He took her virginity. I think their marriage had something to do with that, and she went along with it because she wanted access to an inheritance her mom left her. And to piss off Lennox."

Lennox's jaw clenched. "I found out days ago from Henry. He rubbed it in my fucking face. Talked about how good her virgin pussy was. I stabbed him for it. She was a kid. She was...my best friend." Lennox looked as close to sad as his face allowed, but it was mostly pure anger and hatred for his father.

"Fuck, man. She told me, but she never told me who. If I knew, I would've killed him," I responded. It made so much sense now. Something had always been fishy about what happened between them and their parents and how Amelia hated Lennox despite what her dad did.

"I wanted to just now, but I couldn't. It's not my revenge to get. We have to find her so she can kill him. She deserves to watch the life leave his eyes," Lennox explained. "He's still tied up. I say we go back to Levi's, get one of his men to flip, and then take over his goddamned empire. If anyone disobeys, we simply kill them."

I nodded my head. Lennox's plan wasn't a bad idea. "Maybe

some of Levi's men don't know he deals in sex trafficking. Not everyone's cool with them. Some might turn against him."

"Let's get our guns and get the fuck over there. We need to find her and devise a plan to retrieve her. Someone knows something," Wolf said.

"Already on it, brother," I said, walking toward the locked coffee table, which held several guns and ammo. My fingerprint opened it, revealing a few options for us. We each picked a gun and the corresponding ammo, then headed toward the front door.

One of Levi's top men, Xander, was at the door. Lennox pointed a gun at him, and his hands flew up. "I'm here to help. I know where she's being held. Fuck Levi."

Lennox lowered his gun and pulled the guy in by his shirt. Xander was one of the people there when we first approached Levi's the night she was taken. "Why would you turn against Levi?" Wolf asked.

"I refused to believe he'd kidnap a girl. What reason would he have? So, I looked into it. Levi has a sex-tracking ring in Westpoint. He sells women…including minors. It makes me sick. I can tell you right now who to take out and who will side with you, for the most part."

We exchanged glances with each other, wondering together if we'd trust this man. It was worth it to have the chance to save her.

"I know where she is. I know how we can get men to bring him down. Trust me," he pleaded, his arms still in the air.

"Put your arms down, dude," I directed. "You packing?" I asked.

He pulled up his shirt to reveal a gun in his waistband. "Never leave home without it."

"Let's go make plans," I suggested. "We've got a girl to get back and an empire to take over."

Amelia

My first night in the sketchy cement room led to no sleep. The bed was uncomfortable, the lights were on, and it was cold. Levi promised to send someone into my room today, but I wouldn't know when they'd come. I dreaded knowing someone would touch me. Would Lennox, Cain, and Wolf no longer want me when someone else touched me? They'd never forgive me; I knew it.

The door opened quickly, and two men moved inside. One was Axel, and the other was a man in a suit. I wrestled in my restraints, but it was pointless. Axel smirked at me and shook his head. "You'll never get out of those until it's time to sell you, Raven. Don't hurt your wrists trying. I've brought you a friend."

The man started to remove his suit jacket and unbutton his shirt. His eyes were on me while Axel looked between us. "She's feisty, so we've cuffed her legs. Do whatever you want to her. Just don't bruise her face."

"That's fine by me," he said, removing his tie, freeing himself from his pants, and throwing his clothes to a pile on the floor. He walked to the bed, his hands caressing my legs. "Her body is soft and as delicious as you described." What the fuck was he, a cannibal? I wanted to barf everywhere the minute his fingertips brushed my skin. "She'll do. You may leave," he commanded.

He must've been powerful because Axel immediately left the room, leaving me with this man.

"You're all mine now," he remarked. His face remained blank as if he didn't know how to show emotion. He stood at the edge of my bed, moving my skirt up to expose my bare pussy since I wasn't allowed to wear underwear here. Then, he pushed my top up, exposing my breasts underneath. His fingers pinched my nipples while his free hand began to stroke himself. "I'm going to take it easy on you. You're new, you're cute, and you're not fighting. Lie there and take it, and I won't hurt you. I just need to feel you. They promise me you feel amazing."

Once he's hard, he climbs on top of me, pressing his bare dick to my thigh. He tests me to see if I'll respond, so I take his advice and don't move. Sometimes, being strong means knowing when to listen and knowing when to fight. It wasn't the time to fight. I had a fight in me, but my fight was to get out of here. Hurting him would make things worse for me. I wasn't entirely stupid.

His hand reached between us, and he stroked himself a few times. "You're not wet," he said, frowning.

I shook my head. "My body only gets wet for three men," I responded. Maybe they wouldn't consider it cheating if I told them I couldn't get wet. My body didn't betray me. It couldn't betray me. His touch did nothing to me because he wasn't even skilled. He touched me like he didn't know what a clitoris even was.

When he entered me, I fought hard to hold back tears. The feeling of him sliding inside me while I was dry was painful. His movements were choppy and hurried, his breathing heavy and labored. The smell of whiskey was on his breath, and his

115

grunting sounded like a pig. Sweat began to accumulate on his forehead and drip onto me.

I wanted to scream. I wondered if I could say I was raped if I didn't scream or tell him no. I knew silence was the best option, so I lay there quietly while I let him do his thing. When he left, I knew I'd vomit, but I did a good job of holding it in for the time being. This man didn't seem like he could last long.

"They're right. You feel so good," he groaned.

I memorized his face and body. I made a mental note of every little thing I could: the small mole on his right cheek, the sparse hairs between his brows, the mustache on his face. One day, I'd find his identity, track him down, and kill him. He deserved nothing less. Anyone else that touched me, I'd kill them, too. I felt entitled to that right. Hopefully, my men would find me soon, and no one else would touch me.

If too many did, I'd be tainted. They wouldn't want me anymore.

He lasted two more minutes before he stopped, grunting like a crazed animal as he came. I was glad they forced birth control into my system.

Before he removed himself from on top of me, he pinched my nipple. "Beautiful, perky little tits. Maybe I'll remember you for auction." He grinned before he pulled up his pants, got fully dressed, and walked out the door, leaving me to rot in a painful position on the bed until they sent in someone new for me.

Amelia

I always dreaded the moment the door would open. It meant Levi, Axel, or a stranger was coming in. I could tell how long I had been here by how many men he had sent to my room. He only sent one a day, and today was the fourth. A scrawny blonde man followed him inside. He looked as broken as me.

"This whore needs to be broken in. I remember what you're like. So, break her in. Or you know what'll happen," Levi threatened the guy before patting him on the back and pushing him toward me.

"You can't get away with this," I told Levi. A grin formed on his face. "They'll kill you and Axel. You can't be saved, Levi."

"You overestimate your pussy power, princess. What makes you think I haven't already seen them with someone new?" He left the room before I could respond.

"Do you mean what you said earlier? Someone would kill Levi and Axel to protect you?" the boy asked, scratching his head. He looked like a lost puppy. I tried to judge his age, but it was tough. I assumed he was close to me in age and hoped he wasn't a minor, given his line of work.

"Yes. My men. There's three of them, and they'll kill anyone who touches me," I snarled. Levi told him to take advantage of me. Hurt me. He seemed hesitant to listen. "Violently, too."

"Breathe, Raven. I'm not going to touch you. I don't want to hurt you. We might have to make it seem like something happened, but I promise you're safe with me around," he said. His eyes were glassy and genuine.

"My name...it's Amelia. Call me Amelia," I told him. I didn't want him to call me the name Levi did. "Did they kidnap you too?" I asked in a hushed tone. It was clear he was like me instead of like them. His figure and clothing gave him away. He was skinny, as if he wasn't fed, wasn't well dressed, and didn't seem capable of violence.

He shook his head. "Not in the same sense. They stalked my brother and said they'd hurt me if I didn't do as they wanted. Levi wanted me because I refused to work for him. He promised to teach me a lesson about people telling him no." The thought made me wonder what would've happened to the boys if they rejected him. Instead of threatening those who reject him, he goes like a coward for the ones they love. It's one way to keep people in line. If Levi tells them he has me, they'll stay in line, then scorch the earth to find me. "And I'm Zaidyn."

"You're still here against your will, just like me. I'm sorry. You seem nice...but I don't want to fuck you either," I laughed. "How do we make it seem like we did?"

He climbed on the bed and messed up my hair, so I didn't look like I hadn't moved at all. Then, he removed his shirt and threw it on the floor before hiking up my skirt for me. Levi refused to uncuff me when he sent people into my room. "I don't want to either. You're...not my type. Missing a...certain piece," he choked out before bursting into laughter.

"Thank you for being too gay to want to touch me."

The door burst open, and Levi came through, staring at us

118

angrily. "I'm not fucking stupid," he said. "I'm going to stay here and watch you fuck her, Zai, or I'm going to drag you back and give you thirty whips. Your choice."

Levi had a different game all along. He wanted us to bond, and he wanted to make it hurt.

"Do it, Zaidyn. Please. I can't let you get hurt to defend me," I whispered. He looked pained while he paced around the bed, thinking about his choice. "I want it, please," I said, lying to help him. I could take it, but I couldn't take knowing he got hurt because of me.

Zaidyn climbed on the bed on top of me. It made it easy for me knowing he was gay. He didn't want me any more than I wanted him. I could handle a guy inside me who didn't want to be. It was easier than the men he kept sending to me, who grunted while they released inside me. I was thankful for my birth control shot.

"No," he said, despite looking me directly in the eye while he hovered over me. "I won't do it, Levi."

I watched Levi's face turn red as he grabbed Zaidyn off me, throwing him to the ground. "Fine. If it's dick you want, it's dick you'll get." Levi held Zaidyn to the ground while undoing his belt with one hand. He pulled his pants and boxers down just enough to free his cock, then he pulled Zaidyn's pants down. Except Zaidyn wore gray sweatpants, which I assumed Levi put him in for easy access.

"No! Stop!" I shouted. I couldn't do anything while I was bound to the wall.

Levi didn't prepare Zaidyn before shoving stroking his cock a few times and shoving inside him. Zaidyn faced me, his cheek smashed into the floor as he winced, taking everything Levi forced into him. He shoved into the hilt in his first thrust.

"God, I missed this tight ass," Levi groaned. He pulled out before slamming back in, setting a rough, punishing, and slow pace.

I was forced to watch the pain in Zaidyn's eyes as tears slipped down his cheeks and onto the cold, hard floor. *I'm sorry,* I mouthed. He shook his head. He didn't want me to blame myself.

"I hope it was worth it, Zai. I hope it was worth it to leave her alone, getting fucked by me. It was worth it to me," Levi told him. He reached for Zaidyn's cock and started to jerk it in his hand while fucking him rough in the ass. "I want her to watch you come. I want her to know how weak you are. How you can't control yourself even when you don't want it."

I never thought anything would hurt more than being raped. Watching it happen to someone else hurt worse. I couldn't stop it. What good were my workouts and training if I couldn't use any of the skills I learned?

When Zaidyn reached behind him and gripped Levi's thighs, I couldn't tell if he was getting into it or pretending to be into it.

I could only tell Zaidyn finished by the way Levi broke out into laughter and removed his hand, now covered in cum. I wanted to barf watching him violate someone so sweet, caring, and innocent. Levi needed to die, and I wanted to be the one to kill him.

Levi placed a few slaps on his ass before burying himself inside Zaidyn and finishing with a groan. He pulled out shortly after, catching up on his breathing before pulling up his pants, leaving the kid face-first on the floor.

Levi left the room seconds later after spitting on a broken Zaidyn.

"I'm so fucking sorry," I told Zaidyn.

He got up from the ground with a smile, then dangled a key from his finger. "Don't be." I turned my head since his cock was out, and he quickly remedied the situation by pulling up his pants. "Shit. Sorry." I laughed.

We heard screaming outside the room, and both froze. He quickly walked toward me and undid my wrists from the wall's cuffs, freeing me for the first time in four days. I was stunned and unable to move.

"We can't leave. We have no weapons," I pointed out.

Zaidyn bent down and grabbed something from the floor, then shoved a pocket knife at me. "I've got you covered. This is all you need. Go, get out of here. I need to stay. There's someone I need to see."

I shook my head, refusing to leave him behind. There was no way. Levi would punish him. My thoughts were distracted by more screaming and gunshots. Someone was here, and I only hoped it was my men coming.

"Stay by me," I directed. "I can protect you. If you go out there, I can't. Plus, my men might kill you, but I won't let them."

I heard the door handle jiggle. I put my knife under my leg, and Zaidyn took a step away from the bed.

I expected one or all of the guys to walk in, but instead, I was faced with seeing Levi again. And he looked panicked. His eyes widened when he looked at my freed arms. I smiled the first genuine smile I had since being here. A smile of pure evil because I was giddy for the chance to kill this man.

"Listen to me, Raven, and I won't hurt you," he said, approaching me slowly. "We need to get out of here, now."

"I'm not going anywhere with you. They're here to save me, aren't they?" I asked, cocking my head.

"I won't let them get you. And if you don't willingly come with me, once I take you, I'll make your life even more of a hell," he promised, his eyes darkening.

I laughed. My hand fumbled under my thigh, taking hold of the knife's handle, ready to swing if he took one step closer. "The only person I ever let ruin me is Lennox James. There's nothing you can do to me now, Levi, because I'm going to fucking kill you before you can leave this room."

He chuckled. "With what? Your weak muscles that allowed you to be captured by my men?"

Just like I wanted him to, he took another step forward. My grip on the handle tightened as he stood close, and I jumped up from the bed and rammed the knife into him, sending him rearing back with a knife protruding from his side. "With your own knife."

I walked up to him and grabbed the knife from his side, ripping it away and letting the blood drop to the floor. He grabbed at his side, putting pressure as he screamed in agony. I wanted him to bleed out slowly. I wanted him to be alive when my men came for me.

As if the universe was listening to me, they bashed in the door seconds later. Instinctively, I threw myself in front of Zaidyn. I promised to protect him. Cain led the group, standing with Wolf, Lennox, and other unknown men behind him.

"Little Thorne," he said, glancing between me, Zaidyn, and a floor-ridden Levi. "Tell me right now if this fucker touched you, and I'll end him," Lennox said, stepping in front of Cain. He wasn't looking at Levi; he was looking at Zaidyn.

"No! Leave him be. He saved me," I defended.

"Fine," Lennox said. "Owen, Tobias, take him back to Cain's and get him fed, showered, and dressed," he commanded.

122

They had him out of there before I could speak to protest.

Lennox, Cain, and Wolf entered the room and took in the scene. "You're in the same outfit you went to dinner in," Lennox remarked. "Except it has blood on it now, and your skirt isn't right. What did this fucker do?" Lennox asked, looking at a dying Levi on the floor.

"He raped Zaidyn. He let men rape me. He came for me, so I killed him. Zaidyn freed me and gave me a weapon," I explained.

"Fucking bitch," Levi spat from his spot on the floor, clutching his side.

"I'm going to make sure you're dead," Cain said, stalking toward him. Levi curled into himself.

"No!" I shouted, stepping in front of Cain. "He's already dying. I want to…I want to take back this room…in front of him."

"Are you sure you want that, Little Thorne? I can kill him right now and end his miserable life. We've got his men. We've got his business. His empire is all ours," Cain explained. I sure as shit missed a lot in the four days I was gone.

"Yes. I want to fuck right here, in this bed, and I want you and Lennox to take me while Wolf makes him watch with a knife to the throat," I responded confidently, unsure of why I picked Lennox and Cain. Cain would've gladly held a knife to Levi's throat.

Wolf's eyes widened, and he removed a knife from his pocket, brandishing it for Levi. "My pleasure." I was glad Wolf agreed to my plan. Cain looked hesitant for a moment before sharing a look with Lennox.

"Fine. You want to share us in front of Levi? Then you're going to take both of us in your pussy…at the same time." My breath hitched, and the wetness pooled between my legs for the first time in four days.

Cain

"Get on the bed," I directed Lennox. We were both tops, but when we were with each other, we could flip either way. Right now, I wanted to be in control. I let him take the lead the last time we were together, but now it was my turn. I was about to share the pussy of the woman I loved with one of the men I loved, and if Levi suddenly came to power and killed us all, I'd die a happy man.

But with the knife he had to his throat and Wolf's tight grip, he was done for. He was bleeding out, clutching his bleeding side, but it wasn't helping. He had ten minutes left if he was lucky. As much as I wanted to prolong his death and make him suffer, I'd be happy to have him gone for hurting who we loved.

We destroyed dozens of his men upstairs to get to her. We didn't know this shitty sex dungeon and auction site existed until Lennox tortured the information out of Henry. He must've thought Lennox wasn't going to do anything if he taunted him with Amelia's kidnapping for days. Now, he was missing a few fingers and toes. Lennox left him as a surprise for Amelia. He was hers to destroy.

Lennox obliged, shedding his clothes before lying on the bed, facing upward. I knew the best and easiest way for us to share Amelia. His hand moved up and down his cock slowly a few times until he was hard.

"Do you need me to get you wet, Little Thorn?" I asked, turning to face her. She shook her head.

"Lennox on his back, touching himself while staring at you, does it for me," she said with a hint of lust. "And watching this fucker bleed out," she added, approaching Levi and gripping his hair. "You're going to finally know what it's like when a woman orgasms. Right before you die, you sorry son of a bitch." She spat on him, and the image turned me on. I wondered if anything had happened between them, but it wasn't the time to ask. He'd die either way.

I watched as Amelia walked to the bed, climbed on top, and sat facing Lennox with a leg on each side of him. She impaled herself on Lennox's hard cock without being told. She was still her confident, smart, badass self. She knew what she wanted and went for it. Her mouth fell open in bliss as she slid herself down his length.

"You guys are beautiful together," I murmured, getting closer.

I threw my shirt off. While unbuttoning my pants and pulling them down with my boxers, I leaned down and licked her clit a few times, then moved to where they connected, my tongue covered in the taste of them as his cock rubbed my tongue with each thrust. He moved slowly in and out of her, groaning when my tongue licked him. I loved the taste of both of them mixed. It was two of my favorite flavors mixed together.

"I need you inside me, Cain. Now. Make me feel like you still want me," Amelia pleaded. Did she think I wouldn't want her because other men touched her? She'd never be able to escape us, no matter what.

I hooked my arms under Lennox's legs and pulled them to the edge of the bed. I pushed her forward so her chest was against his, giving me a beautiful view. I lined myself up with her entrance, rubbing in her juices a few times before slowly starting to push inside, my cock rubbing against Amelia's in her body. It was unlike anything I ever felt before. I was stuck in bliss. "I will always want you, Little Thorn. Nothing could get you away from me," I assured her. "You are my Heaven and hell. My savior and damnation. My everything."

"Oh fuck," Lennox moaned. "Your cock feels so good against mine. Fuck her hard, Cain. I want to feel you moving against me." He stilled his movements inside of her, waiting for me to take over.

I gripped her hips and moved inside her to the hilt, watching as she buried her head in his neck and moaned loudly. "Fuck us, Cain. Please. We need it," she begged. I pulled out all the way before slamming back in. Each time, I pulled almost all the way out before slamming back inside, my thrusts slow at first, then starting to build to a faster pace. I watched Lennox's face as he closed his eyes, his hips bucking involuntarily. I smiled to myself, proud of how I could make them feel.

"You feel so fucking good, baby. Both of you," I told them, my hips moving fast and hard, pistoning into them so hard the bed moved with each thrust.

"Stop this. I don't want to see this!" Levi yelled. I could tell when Wolf pressed the knife hard enough to cut because he screamed in agony.

"I'm sick of this fucker. Can I kill him?" Wolf asked. I looked over to see the knife nick his neck with the tip. My fascinated eyes couldn't look away as the blood dripped down his body. The happiness I felt from watching him bleed turned me on more, driving me to fuck Amelia hard. I loved the friction of Lennox's cock each time. I threw my head back in pleasure.

"Choke me," Amelia demanded.

I wrapped my hand around the back of her throat and pressed hard on the sides. Amelia's moans became quieter as I squeezed, stopping when she was on the brink of losing consciousness and releasing to let her breathe. "Just like that," she croaked out. I repeated the process a few more times.

"Christ, I'm going to come so hard," Lennox said between loud pants. "It feels so fucking good."

"Touch Amelia until she comes," I demanded.

Lennox pressed his lips against hers in an aggressive kiss, his finger seemingly working her clit now because she moaned loudly against his lips.

'Kill me now," Levi begged.

"Not until she comes," I reminded him. "Lennox, make her come so we can get rid of this piece of shit."

I heard Levi's scream and subsequent cries fill the room and turned to see Wolf stab Levi in the side. I reached down and pushed a finger into Amelia's ass to help her along. I wasn't sure if reaching orgasm would be hard for her when she spent days likely being raped. I hoped she didn't lose her essence, but I understood if she did.

Amelia clenched around us violently as she pulled her lips away from Lennox's and screamed.

"Oh fuck, oh fuck, oh fuck. It feels so fucking good with you guys inside me," she said. "Cain! Lennox!" Her fingers scratched Lennox's chest, leaving a gorgeous trail of scratches and blood. She orgasmed hard, her pussy gripping us as if it never wanted to let us go. I felt a gush of wetness spraying and looked down to see her squirting all over. I leaned forward, hovering my mouth above her spray and taking it in, drinking down her intense orgasm. "Give it all to me, Little Thorn.

Remember, you belong to us. We'll erase every man's touch," I said, watching as she soaked us and the bed. I rubbed her clit furiously while she squirted, directing the spray all over, letting her soak my chest and face.

"I'm c—coming—Oh, God, I'm coming so fucking hard," Lennox said. His hips bucked up, pushing me deeper inside. I froze, feeling his cock pulse against mine as his warm cum filled her hole.

I heard the knife repeatedly stab Levi, and then Wolf walked over to the bed, standing next to me. "A treat for you," he said, rubbing the cold, blood edge along my nipple. Watching the blood coat me caused me to fill Amelia with my orgasm, a roar tearing from my chest as came harder than I ever had in my life. Feeling him inside of her without a barrier was the best damn feeling, one I wanted to recreate with Wolf later.

I looked over to see Wolf's dead body dropped on the floor, happy with the result.

"Let's get home, get you cleaned up, then repeat this all over again with Wolf," I said to a half-awake, dazed Amelia as she collapsed her weight against Lennox's chest. "Does that sound good?"

"Perfect," she responded. "Let's make sure everyone's out and burn this place to the fucking ground."

"We will. First, we're going to mark you so you never forget who you belong to," I told her, looking at the tattoo gun on the counter.

Amelia

Lennox assured me Henry was alive and in a safe location. We showered, fucked, then showered again at Wolf's before we made our way to Henry's. I had no hurry to look Henry in the eye and kill him. I made time to show my men my thanks after we burned Levi's sex club to the ground. Cain assured me every innocent person got to safety first. When we left, I saw mostly dead bodies, not a single living person. I felt confident in our choice.

"I'm going with you. We all are," Lennox announced before I opened the door to the basement. He gave me a knife when we arrived, too.

"You guys don't think I can be alone with him?" I asked, a snarl of frustration bubbling to the surface. Lennox stepped backward. I appreciated that he didn't underestimate me anymore. He knew exactly who I was and what I was capable of, and he loved me anyway.

"No doubt that you can be, but you shouldn't be. We want to be there for you. We want to watch you kill him," Lennox explained.

I nodded my head, then opened the basement door and walked downstairs. It excited me to see a bloody Henry tied to a chair. A grim smile formed on my face. His slumped head moved up when he heard us enter, and his own devilish grin took over. I refused to look away once we made eye contact. "Hello, Henry."

"Amelia, my broken little flower. Tell me how bad it hurt when the men broke you in. Did Levi drug you? Hurt you?" He laughed. "Tell me all the details. Don't leave one out." Henry was a sick, twisted fuck who got off on the idea of me being broken, but I couldn't break. The only people with the power to destroy me were Lennox, Wolf, and Cain.

"I'm more like a lively flower. I wouldn't say they hurt me, either. I'm fine while you're the one stabbed and bleeding," I pointed out. "Tell me, Henry," I said, walking toward him and pushing my finger into his open thigh wound. "How bad does it hurt? I only wish I was the one who made you bleed."

"You don't want to kill the man who deflowered you, do you?" he questioned. "We hold something special."

I looked toward Lennox to gauge his reaction to things. I was ready to kill his father in a minute, but I didn't want to strain our relationship. Would he view me differently if I killed his dad? Lennox gave me a slight nod.

I raised my knife and moved toward Henry, but his talking halted me.

"Kill me, and you lose my money. You're left with your small inheritance."

"Take off his pants," I directed Cain. He complied, pulling his pants and boxers down to his knees.

"I don't give a shit about your millions, Henry. Neither does your son. We'd rather see you dead, you fuck," I told him, making sure it was clear I was rejecting his money. He thought he would appeal to me by talking about his money from our deal, but no amount of money could keep me from killing him. I would forfeit billions if it meant getting rid of Henry. "I'll see you in hell one day, then I'll kill you all over again." I reached forward and used my knife to slice through his cock, now holding a bloody, soft dick in my hand with a grim smile. Henry screamed, so I put him out of his misery by slitting his throat, making sure the knife cut deep enough for him to bleed out. I could tell he was dead when his body slumped over, held on by the way he was tied to the chair.

Lennox was the first to walk out, and I wondered how he felt. It was one thing to signal you were okay with your girlfriend killing your dad; it was another to watch it happen.

"Go. We'll take care of it," Cain said. I followed Lennox out of the basement.

Lennox

"We need to talk about what just happened," Amelia said, approaching me in my father's bed. "Your dad just died, and your girlfriend killed him. That's a lot." I hoped she didn't think that I cared about that. My father deserved that. I left him for her to destroy. I wanted to kill him when I found out what he did. When he bragged to me about taking her virginity, I stabbed him in the thigh. Then, I wrapped it. I wanted to keep him alive and well enough for Amelia to say whatever she needed.

"I'm glad my girlfriend killed him, okay? When he told me—when he told me what he did, I felt sick. I felt sick that I ever fucking hurt you. I still don't understand my mom's involvement, but you must understand she was the only one who loved me. So, I blamed your father for his actions and took it out on you because he wasn't around. I feel fucking disgusting, Amelia." I had never seen tears in Lennox's eyes until this moment. He didn't seem like the same person I left behind last week.

"I like how you hurt me, Lennox," I admitted. "I didn't like feeling like you didn't love me, but I loved your roughness and how you degraded me." We needed to have an honest conversation about it so he didn't think he needed to change how he handled me sexually. If I hated it before, I wouldn't have let it happen. Cain wouldn't have let it happen. That psychopath wouldn't let anyone genuinely hurt me, not even his best friends.

'There's something you should know, Amelia," he said. He had a pained facial expression on his face. "My mother is dead. She overdosed while you were taken. I love you so much, Amelia. You're my future. Instead of checking on her, I spent my time searching for answers about you, and she's gone." He buried his hand in his palms. I could tell by the vein in his neck that he was trying hard not to cry. It wasn't like him to show emotion. I felt it was time to tell him the truth.

"Your mother knew about what happened to me. You never saw my mom with your dad, and our parents never slept together. My dad raped your mom as revenge. It destroyed your mom, but she didn't care about what happened to me…she blamed me. I think part of why she got hooked on drugs was her guilt about how she handled it. Our dads were always the monsters in our story, but we made it each other instead. They took our letters, tore us apart, changed our phone numbers, and pretended it was us. I…I want to return to my dad's old house and find your letters. They have to be somewhere." I hated the idea of going back to her dad's house. She killed him there, then buried his body in the backyard. He deserved her punishment for what he did to her, selling her to men in a boarding school. All because he learned that having a daughter could be profitable for him.

"There's one more thing," she offered, biting her lip between her teeth.

"You can tell me anything," I whispered. I hoped she felt safe. I could tell she was struggling with what she wanted to say.

"He'd hit me. I thought you knew that and ignored it. I had bruises on me...you never said anything...I thought..." I stopped her, taking her hand in mine and pulling her head to my chest.

"Fuck, angel. I'm so sorry. I was wrapped up in my shit. I stuck with a father who hated me, who I thought I saw fucking my neighbor. I didn't even notice what you were going through."

She rested her head in my lap, and I felt at peace while playing with her hair. "Now that things are going to be different, I need to know you'll still be the Lennox I know and love," she mumbled.

I smirked. Gripping her hair with my fist, I pulled her head up to look me in the eyes. "You want me to be rough with you, baby? Take you right here, right now, with my father's blood still on your body?"

Her shoulders melted into my touch, and she groaned. "Yes, please." I could hear her breath picking up, becoming quicker and shallower. I pulled her lips to mine, fusing our mouths roughly. It felt like I never kissed her enough, especially not before when I treated her like dirt.

"Could've called a guy over," I heard Wolf. I turned around and noticed him in the doorway. I stood up from the bed and walked to him, placing my fingertips on his chest and running them down toward his abs. We had been involved in group activities before, but I wanted a turn with him like Cain. Wolf was the only one I wasn't personally involved with yet. We needed this to finish our group connection and seal us together forever. Wolf needed to know how much he meant to me, too. How sorry I was for all the damage I caused between us.

"We were just getting started. Amelia was just telling me how

135

she wanted me to be rough with her. Come join us," I extended an invite, my cock growing harder in my pants at the prospect of Wolf joining us. I turned around to face Amelia again, and Wolf grabbed my hips, pulling my body flush against his. We watched as Amelia took her shirt over her head and threw it to the ground, then crooked her finger and invited us over.

"I want to fuck you while you fuck her," he whispered in my ear, reaching around my body and gripping the hem of my shirt, taking it off for me. Then, his hands roamed my abs, caressing until his fingers brushed my nipples and pinched. "Be rough with her. I want to watch." He pushed me toward the bed. Amelia took off her skirt and panties while Wolf pushed down my pants and boxers, leaving the two of us naked while he was clothed. "Get her wet and fuck her while I get naked and get you ready to take me."

"I want your tears again, angel. Those innocent, angelic tears turn me on. Though we all know you're far from innocent, aren't you?" I stood at the edge of the bed and pulled her close enough to fuck her. The angle was her favorite. I wanted to prepare her, but she wanted it rough. I could see her glistening pussy, so I knew she was wet enough. "Do you want it rough, angel?" I asked, rubbing my cock up and down her lips to gather her juices. It would help ease me inside her. I wanted to be rough, but I didn't want to cause her harm.

She bit her lip and nodded. "I need it, please. Fuck me," she begged, hitching her legs on my shoulders. I smiled, proud of Amelia. She was never afraid to take what she wanted. She was never afraid to be herself.

I quickly and harshly pushed inside her, watching as her mouth opened at the intrusion. She looked so fucking beautiful every time she took my cock. We gasped together, and I closed my eyes while I basked in the pleasure of her warm, wet pussy squeezing me. I needed a second to get used to the feeling before I went hard on her.

I felt cold, lubed fingers breech my back hole and moaned. I looked back to see a smirking Wolf. "Does that feel good?" he asked, his eyes full of desire and lust for me.

He added a second finger to stretch me, and I moaned, frozen inside of Amelia to the hilt. "Yes," I said, gritting my jaw. It was as painful as it was pleasurable. I never considered taking a cock in my ass before, but now I wish I had done it sooner. It took a minute to get used to it, but it always felt amazing.

I started to slowly push into Amelia again while Wolf worked me hard with his fingers, eventually adding a third. "I'm ready," I told him, turning to look back at him. I tried to show my need with my eyes and hoped it came across that way.

Wolf poured lube onto his hand and stroked his cock a few times. I turned back to Amelia, smiling down at her while Wolf placed his cock at my entrance, the head slowly pushing inside. "Relax for me, baby boy," Wolf said. My head fell forward as he pushed a few more inches inside me. I whimpered, having a newfound appreciation for what Amelia could handle. She took this monster cock regularly, with pride.

"So tight for me," Wolf cooed in my ear. He reached around and pinched my nipple again, causing my slow thrusts to briefly become erratic inside of Amelia while I was overwhelmed with the sensations throughout my body. "Give it to her hard like she asked."

I pulled out of Amelia, and she groaned. "Turn around. All fours." She did as I asked and flipped around, her ass in the air for me. I took fistfuls of her ass and pulled her cheeks apart, slamming my cock inside her pussy again. She moved forward with the motion, her head leaning forward and her forehead resting on the bed as she moaned into the comforter.

"Oh, God. Harder," she pleaded. My girl liked it rough. She called to the dark side of me, and I loved her even more for it.

"Use us," Wolf directed as he stopped moving, a smug smile on his gorgeous face. I knew what he wanted me to do. I slammed into Amelia slowly but fiercely, moving back each time and pushing Wolf's cock into me. I pistoned between them, the feeling on both ends causing me to start moaning. I leaned my head back on Wolf's shoulder, my jaw dropping open as I let pleasure lead me. I didn't go easy on Amelia. I quickened my pace to fuck myself on Wolf's cock hard and fast, enjoying the slapping sounds each time I'd go to the hilt in Amelia and then send Wolf to the hilt inside me.

Wolf's hand slid from my chest to my neck, choking me lightly, which encouraged me to pound into Amelia harder. "Uung—*fuuuck*," I mumbled blissfully, moaning louder as I enjoyed the feeling. "Hurt me, baby. It feels so good." I loved the way Wolf treated me the same way I treated Amelia. Sometimes, I wanted to be used, too.

I moved my head forward again and pressed Amelia's face into the bed, slapping her ass a few times until it turned pink beneath my touch. "Look at that beautiful color."

"Yes, please. More of that. Bruise me." Amelia shocked me. We had never gone hard enough to leave marks on her, but she was asking for it. I could give her what she wanted because I wanted to see her black and blue. I wanted to be the one to cause her pain so I could replace the pain others brought her.

"Suck a beautiful little whore," I told her, smacking her ass harder, repeatedly, then soothing it with a soft rubbing motion. She finally started letting out tears, and they only turned me on further.

"Hold still," Wolf directed. I listened, stopping the movement of my hips with the tip still inside her. Wolf slammed into my ass, hitting deep inside me and pushing me into Amelia. Heaven. We were connected. Wolf moved slowly but hit hard, rubbing against my prostate with each thrust, turning me into a moaning mess.

"Doesn't he feel so fucking good?" Amelia asked, her voice muffled because her face was buried in the comforter.

"God, yes, yes, yes. So good," I agreed. "I'm so close."

Wolf reached for my nipples, giving them a tight pinch. He buried his face in my neck and bit down. A small scream tore from me as I came inside Amelia, Wolf still pounding me ferociously as I did. My cum splattered as it spilled out of her with the force of his thrusts.

"I love making you so messy, baby," Wolf said in my ear.

I could tell Amelia was rubbing her clit by the way her arm shifted, and she started to moan louder. She turned her head to the side, her cheek pressed into the comforter, and she was a beautiful mess of sweat.

"Come, Amelia," Wolf directed.

She fell apart under me, her walls squeezing me to hold on for dear life. I kept being pushed into her, fucking her through her intense orgasm.

"Both of you lay on your knees before me," Wolf said.

We scrambled to do as we were told, getting on our knees before him. He kept stroking himself fast and hard, throwing his head back as thick, hot ropes of cum flew out and landed all over our faces and chest. When he was done, he removed his hand, and his heavy breathing filled the room. He moved and grabbed his phone, taking a picture of us.

"Just for me…and Lennox and Cain," he said, smirking. "Now let's get cleaned up…again," he chuckled. "I think we can all fit in the shower."

Cain

I walked in on Wolf, Lennox, and Amelia fucking, and thought about joining them, but I was inspired to do something else instead: visit my father. It had been a while. He forced us to have monthly dinners. We'd go to a nice restaurant, and he'd give me a check. It was a guilty check— Hush money. I never killed him growing up because I needed him, but I no longer did. Taking over Levi's empire would supply me with enough money to survive without help. I didn't need his house or checks anymore.

He didn't need to live after what he did to me.

He deserved to die.

He lived on the outskirts of town in the most expensive development—one he, of course, built. I hadn't visited in years. The maid, Sarah, wasn't sure how to react when I knocked on the door, but she let me in. She offered me tea, water, or juice while I waited. I said no thanks, and when she returned, I offered her money to leave. She smiled and took it. She knew what I planned. She knew what happened to me.

"Son. To what do I own the pleasure?" he asked sarcastically, walking to his little alcohol cart and pouring himself a whiskey shot. He didn't even offer me anything. He was too selfish. "Need an extra check this month? Or are you ready to talk about taking over the company?" He walked to a table and grabbed his checkbook. I chuckled. He thought every problem related to money in one way or another. And he had told me he wanted me to take over his empire. It was ironic that I now took over someone else's. I was in college to study business and real estate since he paid for it, but I had no genuine interest. I hardly even attended classes.

Bossing around people, selling drugs, and killing people? I have an interest in that.

"No, no. Actually, I just took over Levi's business. And we'll be cutting ties with you," I said. All of our fathers worked with Levi in some capacity. They had to. Anything illegal that happened in this town went through him.

My father scoffed. "Levi and I have worked on our relationship for years. You won't be doing shit," he said sternly.

I chuckled. "Levi is dead. Amelia stabbed him; then Wolf finished the job while I was fucking Amelia with Lennox."

His face paled, his thin lips straight as his face turned red. "All that training, and you still enjoy fucking around with men? Scum like Lennox?"

I reached into my waistband and put my hand on the gun, prepared to pull it out and shoot him at any moment. As much as I loved bloodshed, I needed to make this look more legit. I couldn't be a suspect.

"Lennox is twice the man you'll ever be. You let disgusting men fuck your son when he was a child. It taught him nothing; it only brought him trauma and pain. What kind of fucking father does that?" I asked. "I love Lennox, Wolf, and Amelia. And I'm happy that you'll never be around for the birth of your grandchild. I'm going to drop the Maddox name entirely and destroy Maddox Investments. You'll be nothing, Dad." A grim smile took over my face. For once, I felt at peace. I wondered if Amelia felt this sense of relief before she killed her own father.

"You won't do jack shit, you ungrateful little shit. I did everything for you!" He stepped toward me, and I pulled out my gun. I aimed it straight at his chest and pulled the trigger three times, making sure he was done and not breathing before I considered walking away. "Fuck you, daddy dearest," I said. I'd spit on his face if I weren't worried about my DNA.

I walked out the front door and handed money to the two men out front. I paid them to make it look like a robbery gone wrong. I left the house while hearing the sounds of things crashing and being thrown everywhere, and nothing made me happier.

He was gone. My monster was destroyed.

Amelia

My first night sleeping after Henry's death and my kidnapping was an absolute nightmare. I gave up his house and money, leaving me at my old house, but it was no longer the same. This house was given to me as a way to lure me into town. Henry was manipulative and working behind the scenes. He wanted me because he chose me as a child. He felt I owed him because he stole my virginity, and my dad raped his wife. In a weird way, he cared about her. What my dad did destroyed her. I had a hard time caring, knowing how much it destroyed my own mother.

Everyone who deserved to suffer for what they did, did. Henry and my father both died from my hand. Lennox's mom overdosed while I was kidnapped. Lennox knew the entire truth now. Henry admitted most of it to him, and I filled in the blanks. Once I came clean about everything, he said he refused to hold a funeral for either of his parents. Cain, Wolf, and I were the only family he needed.

Wolf was the only one with a dad who was still alive. So, we agreed we'd all meet him. Wolf's dad allegedly accepted our relationship status, but I wasn't sure I believed him yet. I'd need to see how he treated us firsthand.

We met with Cain's new team before we headed to the

location Wolf's dad sent us. The new men were eager to work with Cain since he was a much more understanding boss than Levi. He never forced anyone to do what they didn't want to and gave people choices. He increased their profits for drugs sold and wiped the debts of people who were working with Levi just to keep their family alive.

Cain was generous, leading a new lifestyle for criminals that made their lives better. He enjoyed what he was doing now.

He refused to take Levi's house, so he gave it to the newest member of his team, who had been homeless before, Zaidyn. Zaidyn cried. He also left him a fridge full of food since Zaidyn spent months eating only one meal a day. They were cool with him once they sat down with Zaidyn and understood the situation better. They felt bad for him and wanted to help take care of him. If he weren't gay, I wouldn't have already claimed him for my harem.

"This isn't my dad's house," Wolf said as we approached the nice, two-story, white-bricked house. It was a new build, but one that Cain's dad wasn't building. "At least not that I know of. He moved after Mom's death so I wouldn't have to step foot in the house ever again, but the address doesn't match."

Wolf's dad was standing outside, waving at us and smiling. "That's definitely your dad," I said. We exited the car and walked toward him as he stood outside the house.

"Whose house is this?" I asked, looking up at the beautiful building accented in black. "It's lovely."

Wolf's dad smiled. "You must be Amelia. I've heard a lot about you. I'm glad my son found you." He shook my hand, and I awkwardly smiled. I had never met someone's parents before. "Boys, it's glad to see you again," he said, hugging Cain and Lennox.

"Dad, you failed to answer the question," Wolf pointed out. His dad chuckled, then brought him into a hug.

"I heard what happened to all of you, and I felt so bad that you had shit parents. But, you helped my son come back to me. You loved him when he felt unworthy of love. You loved him while he battled demons he couldn't tell me about," he said, a few tears falling down his cheeks, "I need you to know how grateful I am, how supportive I am of your relationship. I figured you would all want to start over and move on from your houses, so I bought one for you all to share. There's even a custom-built double king bed in the master," he explained. "I don't own it. It's all in your names," he finished, reaching into his pocket and handing us each a key.

My jaw dropped in utter shock. I didn't know Wolf's dad, but he went to great lengths to show us he cared, and that meant a lot to me. Growing up, I didn't have a good father figure, but I finally found a grown man I could trust.

"Wow, Dad, thank you. Seriously, this means so much to us," Wolf said, bringing his dad in for a giant hug. It was a heartwarming moment. One Cain, Lennox, and I had never experienced. I squeezed their hands, reminding them we had each other. We never needed anything more.

"Let me show you around the place," he offered. "You're going to love it."

Epilogue

Amelia
One Year Later

I left my appointment happier than ever. After the boys forced me to take birth control, I decided to keep taking it, but from a legitimate medical professional. My last dose worse off recently, and I asked her about the ability to conceive. She said I was on it for so short of time that I might be able to conceive within weeks of stopping. Or else it'd take a few months, which wasn't bad. Apparently, it only took weeks.

We all dropped out of college last year. Wolf, Lennox, and Cain attended to make their fathers happy. I went because I wanted to do something with my life but didn't need college. The boys were off running a criminal empire, and I wanted nothing more than to be a mother. Of course, I wasn't ready until now, so I spent my time writing a book on my story with the three men I loved.

It was a hit. It turns out that suburban moms love dark romance stories in which a woman gets railed by three men. Who knew?

I hit the goal number that I gave them for when I decided we'd try for a baby, but I hadn't yet told them I stopped my birth control. I wanted to surprise them. I told them we'd have a celebration tonight, and they agreed to make a meal for me, but I haven't told them what we are celebrating yet.

I sat outside the house in my car, smiling down at my ring finger with their initials tattooed around it—the mark they left last year after finding me.

I came home to a dimly lit house with the smell of spaghetti filling the air. It smelled divine. Spaghetti and meatballs were Cain's signature meal. Each of the guys had their own—Lennox had meatloaf, and Wolf was great with steak. Part of what made Cain's spaghetti special was his homemade sauce and garlic bread. I loved the fresh smell throughout the place. It was like an aphrodisiac to me.

I walked into the dining room, and the place was set up with four plates. The spaghetti and garlic bread were already on the plates, and my men sat around the table with a seat open for me. I sat next to Lennox, with Cain and Wolf across from us. "It smells and looks amazing," I said.

We started to eat, and Cain passed around glasses of wine. I looked up at him with a smile and shook my head. I didn't want any on this special night.

Cain's eyes widened. "Is that what we're celebrating?"

I bit my lip and nodded. "I stopped my birth control several weeks ago. I didn't want to say anything in case my plan didn't work, but I'm pregnant," I announced. Everyone dropped their forks and jumped from their seats, running to my side. They hugged me, making me feel warm and happy. I knew I belonged with them. I wouldn't change anything about our relationship, but I wish I could change the trauma we had to experience to get here.

"Is this why you've only accepted triple penetration for

weeks?" Wolf asked, blushing. I knew his dad would be beyond excited to hear about the news. Maybe he'd finally have his future security firm owner he always wanted since Wolf didn't want the job.

"We agreed to have a baby with all four of us, so we never questioned the father. As far as I'm concerned, you're all the father. Maybe your sperm mixed or something," I joked. I was pretty certain that wasn't possible, but I could pretend in my head. "I'm going to tell a few people who deserve to know. Then, we'll really celebrate." I winked before I walked off. I took my phone out of my pocket and texted my group chat with Lily and Zaidyn, letting them know the news. They were my best friends. Both of them would be beyond happy. Since we spent so much time together, they were practically Uncle Zaidyn and Aunt Lily.

"I think we've got a few more positions to explore before you get too big," Cain teased, leaning in the doorway.

I turned to face him. He grinned, walked toward me, picked me up, and threw me on the bed. 'Then we better get started," I replied, my eyes shifting to Wolf and Lennox in the doorway.

Stay Tuned

Looking for an extra scene of Amelia and her men or the story of Zaidyn and his? Join my Facebook group, Ashley Reyes's Dark Hearts, to keep updated! This isn't the end for these characters.

Acknowledgments

This book wouldn't exist without the people encouraging me every day. Thank you to anyone who has sent a kind message. I write for you.

A massive thank you to every beta reader who gave me feedback, especially Jen, Colbi, and Katarina, for leaving many notes. You caught things my eyes missed several times. This book would've been a hot mess without you all.

I appreciate any and all who have supported me in any way. You keep me motivated and going, so thank you.

About the Author

Ashley is a new author living in Nashville, TN with her fiancé, three guinea pigs, and a bunny. When she's not writing or reading, she's probably playing a video game, or photographing a concert. She enjoys reading dark romance, contemporary romance, and romantasy.

You can connect with me on:
- https://ashleyreyesauthor.com
- https://www.tiktok.com/@ashleyreyesauthor
- https://www.instagram.com/ashleyreyesauthor

Printed in Great Britain
by Amazon

41298083R00091